The
Franklin Project

Debrah Dennis

Fulton Books, Inc.
Meadville, PA

Published by Fulton Books 2020

ISBN 978-1-64654-764-7 (paperback)
ISBN 978-1-64654-765-4 (digital)

Printed in the United States of America

DEDICATION

This book is dedicated to the women who survived trauma when they had no control or choice. We did survive, and we do go on. But we can also find comfort in imagining revenge.

CHAPTER 1

Caron

Caron pried up a loose worn board under a chair in her kitchen to grab some money for her trip to work. She had not trusted anyone in an exceptionally long time and learned to conceal everything of value, even her day-to-day cash. She needed to make the 11:00 a.m.– 7:00 p.m. shift at the grocery store across town but had overslept her alarm.

Caron's abused body needed the extra sleep after her most recent encounter yesterday evening. She had battled two men wielding what appeared to be brand-new claw hammers. She had been walking home from the corner store on an unseasonable, warm fall evening when they tripped her to the ground and pounded her body to subdue her quickly. She watched through dazed eyes as the contents of her grocery bag spewed on a strip of grass between the road and the sidewalk.

The men then picked her up and carried her down an alley behind the old run-down row homes of her neighborhood with intentions of doing more harm. It was there that Caron seized her opportunity to gain control. When they were satisfied with the location, they released her, and in that split second, Caron jumped to her feet and disarmed one of the attackers.

Man number one immediately fled, and she then faced man number two with a bloodied hammer now in her hand. The second man swung his hammer to strike Caron, but she sidestepped his attempts until she was able to grab his wrist and pound her hammer on his hand. He howled loudly in pain and dropped his hammer, which fell on the ground at Caron's feet. Caron released his arm, and he, too, fled as though he were the victim.

Having escaped, Caron went down the alley and back around to the front of the row homes. She leaned against one of the old oak trees that lined the street for a moment to calm her racing heart and collect her wits. On the ground lay her few groceries—a half-gallon of milk, bread, muffins, tortilla chips, and gum. She picked them up and stuffed them as best as she could back into the torn plastic shopping bag.

Her wrist and leg throbbed with pain as she slowly limped herself the few blocks home over the broken-up sidewalk of her neighborhood. There were people on their front porches, smoking cigarettes and shooting shit, and Caron wondered if any of them were aware of what just occurred.

She realized she still had the bloody hammer in one hand and threw it to the ground, not caring one little bit if the neighbors saw it. Or if they saw that her short blond hair was disheveled, appearing to make her five-feet-four-inch frame appear taller as the wind whipped it upward. People in her neighborhood always minded their own business when it came to street violence.

Caron pushed away the self-pity again. She had already assessed her bruised hands and knew there would undoubtedly be questions at work. No one ever believed her explanations, so she stopped telling the truth about her attacks. Instead she offered different excuses each time, like she was a battered spouse: "I tripped on the steps," "I slammed my fingers in the door," "I fell off my bike," etc. Surely her coworkers believed she had an abusive boyfriend by now, but it beat hearing the snarky remarks that she made up another story, probably just looking for attention, probably just lonely, quite the imagination on that girl. None of which was helpful and only further alienated Caron, who fought to keep from going into the depths of depression. She had accepted long ago that she would always be on her own to deal with these attacks, but that did not make things easier.

As Caron rose from the floor, she realized it was not just her hands that were sore, her whole body hummed with slow, throbbing pain. She opened the cabinet above her kitchen sink to get a bottle of ibuprofen and popped four into her mouth, hoping to ease the discomfort before work. She knew she would have to suck it up if she was to make the 10:30 a.m. train to Owings Mills and her job at the Shopper's Supermarket there. Being late again would mean a write-up and another ding to her employee record. Something she needed to avoid almost as much as the street men. She needed this job badly.

Caron poured coffee into a to-go cup and grabbed a pumpkin muffin and ran out into an overcast fall morning with leaves falling like a gentle rain. The breeze and leaves soothed her soul, as she loved this time of year. She felt a small rejuvenation of her spirit with the chilly air after the warmth of last night, a sure sign that the last breaths of summer were being exhaled.

She managed to make the train just as the doors thudded closed. Settling into her seat, she began the process of thinking through her workday. She knew a new shipment of fruit had arrived that needed to be shelved. She wondered how bad the broccoli and green beans would be as they were high-volume sellers and on sale this week. Later in the day, she would need to sanitize the potato bins, as apparently someone saw mold underneath and reported it to the store manager. Breezing through the door with a fake smile in place, Caron greeted Ms. Kelly at the register and began her day.

In the produce cooler, Caron loaded a cart with squash and was pushing it through the swinging doors when Eddie, her coworker, bumped into her. Caron let out a small whimper, and Eddie pounced as predicted. She immediately regretted whimpering, as Eddie would always ask her questions designed to figure out her homelife. She fully realized Eddie thought she was abused and was unable to bring herself to tell him her truth.

"Caron, what's going on? Looks like you smashed your hand again. You okay?" Eddie asked.

Caron smiled and said, "Of course. You know me, the store klutz," then pushed past him onto the store floor.

He followed closely beside her and said, "You do know that if you ever need anything, I'm here for you, right?"

Caron turned and looked at her handsome tall coworker and said, "Eddie, you are a worrywart. Go back to work."

She laughed to add some authenticity and moved along to stock her squash.

Eddie was a good guy, and Caron felt sure she would have asked him for help had domestic abuse been her issue. She wished it were. Then at least she would know what was coming. Caron managed her workday without any more whimpers and punched out promptly on time.

CHAPTER 2

Later that night, as she lay in bed, Caron wondered, as she had so many times before, *Why me? Why am I always involved in so many altercations?* She thought about that first trip to the corner grocery store to buy milk when she was nine, almost ten years old.

The store was only a couple of blocks away, but Caron felt like an older and newly independent girl being allowed to go alone. She was surprised her mother would even permit this. She was lost in the excitement and was skipping along the familiar pavement when an older boy pulled her into an alley and punched her so hard in the belly that she lost her breath. He stole her money and made her take off her clothes and stole those too. Her protest was met with another fist, so she laid whimpering in the alley naked, ashamed, and scared.

Later when the police and doctors were done and returned Caron home, her parents sent her to bed crying instead of being supportive. She found them the next morning zoned out on the sofa, high once again.

Even at an early age, Caron understood her parents had a drug dependency issue. She tried desperately to shake her mother awake then her father, but both were completely unresponsive. Feeling utterly lost and alone, Caron went back and laid in her bed, terrified and crying until she fell asleep again.

For many years to come, sleep would be her only escape. It provided Caron the solace she did not get from her parents after any of her attacks. In her sleep, no bad guy could hurt her. Caron would not allow them in. Instead she learned to deliberately dream of a happy life, one where she could eat cake any time she wanted or could have a soft and cuddly puppy to crowd her in her small bed at night.

Caron liked it best when she dreamed of both her parents holding her hands and walking down the middle of an amusement park. They would be looking up in awe at all the lights and sounds the rides generated, deciding which ride to try first. She had heard her classmates talk about the fun they had at Kings Dominion, and she wished desperately her parents would take her. But it never happened.

Caron's parents were trash and, to put it bluntly, vile and disgusting. They were both heroin addicts with sporadic periods of sobriety that never lasted more than a few months. Caron would live for those in-between months when her mother would cook a real dinner or fix a lunch for her to take to school or even do her laundry. Caron would deeply love her mother during those periods, only to have her heart shattered once again. And it always seemed to Caron that when she needed them the most, they would be strung out and oblivious. She had learned ways to cope on her own after every attack over the years, and by the age of sixteen, she no longer had love for her parents.

Shortly after her sixteenth birthday, Caron began to plan for her escape from home and the ugly life she felt she was trapped in. In her gut, she knew the change was necessary for her mental health and her desire to be happy. She decided to steal any cash she could find the next time she found her parents strung out, and she would get away. At the time, Caron was uncertain of what her destination should be but knew she needed to put a plan in place. She opened the map app on her phone and randomly decided she would go southeast and be a beach bum. Her thought process was *Why not?* At least she could see the ocean and listen to its calming waves crashing the shore whenever she wanted. She would find a job that did not require previous work experience, like cleaning hotel rooms or waiting tables. That settled, she knew she needed to wait for the right opportunity. *To hell with them*, she thought at the time. William and Sonya Tucker were worthless human beings and even more worthless parents.

The following week, after Caron put her escape plan together, she had another random attack that she once again had to deal with on her own. Being raped for the third time took its toll on Caron, and it was the last straw for her and her parents.

The next morning, Caron clearly saw her opportunity and stole eight hundred dollars from her mother's dresser drawer. She watched as her parents danced around their small row home to unheard music, high again.

She stuffed only what was necessary of her belongings into a duffel bag, along with the money she stole, and let the screen door slam loudly as she left, knowing her parents could care less. She managed to hitchhike her way to Ocean City, Maryland, where she would live for the next two years waiting tables and without a single attack.

In Ocean City, Caron managed to get paid under the table and carefully hid her money behind the small refrigerator of the efficient apartment where she lived with three other girls. But she lost all her savings the day she returned to Baltimore, her cursed city.

Caron knew she needed a better job than the scraps she made in Ocean City, and Baltimore was the only other town she knew, so she headed home. Upon her return, she was ill prepared for the sudden attack and the loss of all her funds with her clothing in the duffel bag. She reported the mugging at the police station in hopes of recouping the stolen money but was advised by a detective that she would never see it again.

She was feeling defeated, again, when the detective suggested Caron should check out a women's shelter nearby. Feeling desperation taking hold, she took the detective's suggestion and walked the six blocks to the old armory building that housed the shelter.

The women who ran the shelter were incredibly helpful for Caron, who was enormously grateful. She needed a break. They helped her get some clothing to hold her over then advised her of an open position at the Shopper's Supermarket for the produce department. Caron was just nineteen then, and seven years later, she still worked at that Shopper's.

CHAPTER 3

About five and a half years ago, when she was twenty, Caron vowed to herself to become deadly. She would have to harden her resolve and learn to defend herself so that she would no longer be a victim. She worked extra hours whenever possible at the Shopper's to afford this defense training and took it very seriously.

Her journey of learning to skillfully fight back was working, as her last two attacks were decidedly big victories. Caron smiled, knowing she was finally taking control of her own safety. It was well past the time for her to decide what happens herself and put a stop to these never-ending attacks.

RAM's Gym was in a strip shopping center, a few miles from Caron's apartment. RAM got its name from the owners, Reggie and Mike, and was furnished with newer equipment and offered excellent self-defense classes. The owners prided themselves on having well-maintained equipment and a clean gym environment, which was appealing to Caron. Caron entered the gym, her second home these past few years, and began her warm-up on a punching bag.

Reggie Jones was Caron's primary strength and conditioning coach. Reggie was a bald Black man, short at five feet, five inches but as strong as an ox from years of working the weights. Reggie was also a curious man and sought to learn trivial things. Most of these things he stored for later use to provide examples as he trained his athletes.

One day, he shared a story of how he once bet on a cockroach race because he had read somewhere that the darker-colored ones were significantly faster than the paler ones. Clearly, that was not true, as he handed over a hundred dollars when the pale cockroach ran a crooked path but still crossed the finish line first. His example meant to support the saying, "You can't judge a book by its cover."

But when it came to Caron, nothing was trivial to him. He understood Caron's desire to not only feel safe, but to ensure her own safety.

Reggie worked Caron hard, as he had once worked himself hard for similar reasons. Reggie had been bullied when he was younger because of his size. As a kid, he was scrawny and always the shortest one, but he had been determined to stop the bullying by bulking up, which, of course, he did.

After a brief break from the weights and conditioning, Caron headed back to Mike Heller for the second half of the day's training. Mike was undeniably the lethal half of this training team.

Being a former Navy SEAL, Mike had the best of the best training with hand-to-hand combat and the technical skills Caron desired to have herself. Mike was a tall, White man, strong but not muscle-bound like Reggie. His light-brown hair was cut so short you could not tell if it was naturally curly or straight. Quiet and unassuming by nature, you would never expect what Mike was capable of inflicting, though he was never boastful. His unspoken confidence convinced Caron he was the man for the job when they first met. She felt Mike would be her salvation. It was the reason she worked so many hours to pay him.

In recent weeks, Caron had become quite adept at escaping and defending herself under Mike's guidance, but she could and wanted to get better. Sure, she had won the last couple of battles but only barely. And not without damage, as her latest bruises proved.

"Hello, Mike."

"Hello, Ms. Caron. You ready for today?" Mike responded then began to take in the bruises on Caron. "Please tell me Reggie worked you too hard," he said.

Caron smiled and winked. "No, but you should have seen the other guys," she said, fully aware of her corny response.

She then laid out the previous night's event for Mike. He briefly went over her tactics and offered advice on being more aware of the possible dangers. He put the attack aside and moved on to Caron's newest lesson.

This was the day Caron had been looking forward to for weeks. Mike would introduce weapons for the first time, small firearms specifically. Caron was excited to learn her way around the .45 mm semiautomatic that Mike pulled out from his bag.

There's power in wielding that thing, she thought as she gave her full attention to the day's lesson.

Mike went over the basics of safety and cleaning then let her target shoot. Caron did quite well for her first attempt at shooting. In the coming weeks, Mike would add some pressure and distraction, as she needed to be able to handle herself under duress. He would suddenly yell or push her or fire off a round himself without warning, all designed to put her on edge. He would make her stop, disassemble her firearm, and then reassemble again. Then he made her do it all over again until her fingers were too sore to continue. Mike would push Caron at every session until she cried uncle and ended the session, completely spent.

Mike continued to drill Caron this way until she had nerves of steel. Caron could tell Mike was proud of her accomplishments and told her as much. She believed she was an excellent student, and Mike ensured she would be empowered to take control of any situation by the time her training concluded. It was the whole reason she hired him.

Those dollars spent on training were a hardship for Caron, so she took notice of the flyer stapled to the telephone pole on her walk home from the gym that day. She knew she needed another source of income if she was to continue training at this level with Reggie and Mike.

The flyer said, "Are you looking for an exciting career in defense? We offer paid training to the right candidates." *Interesting,* she thought, then quickly dismissed the idea, thinking they would never consider a short woman anyway. That was a job for a man. Caron was already well aware that the world did not think of women as equals to men. Certainly it would be rare for a woman to be in this field.

Back at home, Caron guzzled a protein shake and then ate a huge dinner of chicken, rice, and green beans. She found that lately she was always hungry, especially after the intense trainings with Mike like she had today. She also was always ready to drop in bed and sleep. So after a long, hot bath, she laid in her bed and flipped on the TV to see if anything good was on. Her body had another idea and now welcomed the rejuvenation of a good night's sleep.

CHAPTER 4

Several weeks had now passed, and Caron continued working at the grocery store and with her training with Reggie and Mike. She began to relax as normalcy finally seemed to be taking over her life and confidence began its grip. As her workouts further intensified, she realized she no longer had the insane end-of-day fatigue. Her body was adjusting to this routine very well.

She still needed to eat an enormous number of calories, but she was managing to sneak in raw veggies as she stocked the store shelves at work. That helped with the grocery bill and with the newfound diversity of her diet. Caron would never have eaten squash or beets or yellow peppers, especially raw, had they not been part of her day at work. Not only did she eat them now, but she enjoyed them and looked for every opportunity to sneak into the bathroom and wash a freshly "broken" pepper.

Clocking out at work one day, she noticed that same flyer for a career in defense again. It was posted on the community corkboard next to the punch clock, and this time she read it in its entirety.

CAREER IN DEFENSE

Are you looking for an exciting career in defense?

We offer paid training to the right candidates.

We will train and supply you everything necessary for the position.

Women are strongly encouraged to apply.

Must be willing to travel.

Call for more information.

This time, she attempted to tear off the number on the tabs at the bottom but instead got the whole paper. What could it hurt? She would give them a call when she got home and find out exactly what this was about.

*****

Caron stepped out into the dark evening with the advertisement in hand, imagining what it could be about. She folded it and put it into her jacket pocket for safekeeping.

Walking to the train station, she mused, *Secret agent? Special police? Secret Service? Night guard at the grocery store?* She laughed out loud and muttered, "Can you imagine me—a skinny, short blonde—doing that?"

And then everything went black.

CHAPTER 5

Caron woke up and realized she was being driven in a van. She had no idea how long she had been unconscious but felt it was a brief period. Her hands were bound in duct tape.

She peeked around to take in her situation without alerting her abductor, one man—heavyset, glasses, and ball cap, baseball bat by his side, dirty windows, coffee cup, and rope under the passenger's seat. She tried to see street signs but was unable to do so; they were not on a highway. There were no windows in the back of the van either. And now they started on a gravel road.

Caron was scared, but a calm overtook her as her training kicked in. Escape was her primary goal. She remembered the trick Mike showed her on how to get out of duct tape and decided to save that for when her abductor exited the van to come around to get her. Having patience was agonizing, as was pretending to still be unconscious, but Caron formulated her plan and waited for the right time to act.

The van slowed and came to a gentle stop. Caron closed her eyes, knowing he would look back at her before exiting. She heard the door open and peeked as he grabbed the bat and a knife from the dash. She had not been able to see the knife.

Her heart raced as she knew she was about to launch into action. When she heard the door close, she sat up, snapped her hands apart, and grabbed the rope from under the seat. Then she gently slid up against the side wall by the back door, hoping he didn't hear her movements. The door swung open, and Caron pounced immediately, striking the butt of her hand directly into his nose, causing an audible break.

Stunned and blinded with pain, the man fell backward, dropping both the knife and bat. Caron jumped on him and wrapped the rope around his neck and scooped up the knife. He pleaded with her not to kill him.

She took his wallet from his pocket and took his license out: John James Smith.

"Well, Johnny boy, you just sit right here while I call the police," Caron said.

Completely bewildered, Johnny boy did not move a muscle, surely relieved he was not going to die this day.

Caron popped his license into her pocket for her future consideration. At the back of her mind, she always thought there was something to her attacks, and maybe this would be evidence.

Caron recognized the gravel lot where they were parked. It was a small construction site a few miles from her job. She phoned 911, and the police arrived moments later, followed by an ambulance. After convincing the EMTs she could take care of her probable concussion, she watched their taillights disappear back down the gravel road.

Caron settled into the back of the police cruiser for a ride back home. She looked again at the ID she had taken off her attacker and decided to check out his home first thing tomorrow morning. Perhaps she could gather some insight into this man and find out if he was somehow connected to all her attacks. This was the first time Caron was able to get any kind of information off an attacker and the first time the police were able to make an arrest. The tables felt like they just might be turning for Caron.

Thank you, Mike Keller, she thought. *You are worth every dime spent.*

CHAPTER 6

Emptying her pockets as was her habit when returning home, Caron dropped her keys and wallet in a basket and tacked the employment flyer to her refrigerator door with a magnet.

"Man, am I tired," Caron lamented the next morning. *Why must my life need to exist in this survival mode? I need to live easier and more relaxed,* she thought. *I want to breathe easy and not need to be on edge all the time.*

Pouring a cup of coffee and having a seat at her table, Caron began to think again about the flyer she had tacked up on her fridge.

Why not? At the very least, it really cannot hurt to see what this notice is about. But first, Johnny boy needs to be looked in to.

She fingered the ID that was already in her pocket. That was this morning's mission.

Caron wanted to get to his home quickly in case Johnny made bail. She was sure she did not have a concussion this time. No headache and no nausea. At least, there was that. She ate a banana and gulped down the rest of her coffee and headed out into a spectacular sunrise. The weather, once again, soothing.

Caron's plan was to first jog past the house to see if anyone was at home. The house was set back off the street and was completely dark. Hopefully that meant Johnny had not yet made bail. She ran around the block and cut through to Johnny's backyard and quickly climbed the steps of the deck.

She peeked inside and saw it was a kitchen, but otherwise, nothing happening, complete stillness. It would be perfect if he lived alone in this big house. She pried at the bottom of a sliding door to release the lock and slid it open.

You would think a person who commits crimes would at least know better than to not have a safety bar on a sliding door. Dumb criminal, she thought as she looked up into the wide eyes of a girl about six years old. *Oops. Johnny boy had a family.*

Caron smiled at the little girl and backed out of the house, slid the door closed again, and disappeared the same way she came. This will have to happen another day. Or not at all. She worried that she would cause emotional harm to the little girl. There was enough of that to go around, and Caron was not feeling like sharing.

Since she was already dressed in her running gear, Caron decided to get her daily run out of the way. She had six miles to do as she always did on a weekday. Weekends were different though. Then she would clock in ten or fifteen miles, depending on how she felt. There was something to that runner's high, and sometimes she just did not want to come down.

As she ran through the raining leaves, Caron kept in mind Mike's lessons of being aware. She needed to know if someone was running behind her. She needed to spot the person hiding behind a building at the end of the block peeking out, waiting. She needed to notice the man who would suddenly jump off a bench and start to run. She needed to see the whole picture, as Mike put it.

Listening to her own sneakers pounding the pavement, Caron continued into mile four, where she spotted just such a person. He was leaning on a tree. Why? She questioned his very existence as she cautiously approached, fists at the ready. His eyes seemed to be closed. Could be a false alarm, another dope addict doing the "lean," as they called it in Baltimore. He was using the tree to prevent himself from falling on the ground. She safely ran past the leaner and continued, awfully glad that he was just that.

CHAPTER 7

Back at home, Caron cooked four scrambled eggs and some bacon, then mixed them together before wolfing them down with her coffee. She had a lot on her agenda today. More specifically, she needed to clean. It had been a couple of months since Caron took the time to stop and get her place back to the neat and clean place she used to keep before all the training began.

She had noticed that it was becoming evident that she pried up the board under her kitchen table, and she wanted to put a fresh coat of wax down to hide the scratches. She changed into some old shorts and a T-shirt and set about righting the place.

There will never be anyone else entering my apartment, she thought but hoped she was wrong.

Caron had lately been dreaming of meeting a man to ease her loneliness, someone to hang out with and talk about sports or music or TV shows or anything. Eddie was the closest thing to a friend she had, and he had never set foot in her place. She should invite him over to watch a Ravens' game. It would be nice to hang out and get to know someone better. Her confidence had grown enough that this might be possible for her now.

Caron stood back and admired the shine on the floor and decided she would indeed invite Eddie to this Sunday's game.

It will be great to feel like a normal person, she thought.

She would ask him as soon as she started her 6:00 a.m. shift tomorrow. Tonight though would be all about some wine and a movie and being lazy. *Shawshank Redemption* was on again, and Caron never got tired of that movie. She popped some microwave popcorn for the occasion and settled back into the headboard of her bed to watch.

Thank God Caron had the foresight to set her alarm when she started the movie. She woke to its blaring car horn sound with popcorn stuck in her hair. No wine spilled though. That was good. She rose and hit the shower to prepare for her workday, practicing in her head how she would approach Eddie and invite him to the game tomorrow. She settled for just straight up asking.

With coffee in hand, as usual, she headed outside for the long walk to work. The train did not run early enough for her 6:00 a.m. days, so instead she made the trek by foot. She noted sadly that most of the leaves had fallen, and soon winter would take its hold.

As much as Caron loved the autumn, she hated winter. Always did. The cold, freezing rain, snow, ice? All of them sucked. The only saving grace was the quiet. Birds flew south. Rabbits hibernated. Idle squirrels just nesting until they needed one of their stashed acorns. So if there was a noise, it was usually hushed.

*****

Caron was loading up a cart of potatoes that were on sale when Eddie breezed through the doors, tying his apron as he walked.

"Good morning!" he said cheerfully.

Caron responded, "Back atcha. Got plans for the Raven's game tomorrow? Want to watch with me?"

And just like that, she blurted out her invitation.

Eddie's eyebrows raised in surprise.

"I would love to, Caron, but I'm thinking my wife would not appreciate the female companionship."

Caron blushed. She had not known Eddie was married and quickly acknowledged that and offered her apology. Eddie, always the good-hearted guy, seemed to take it in stride and let her off the hook.

"I genuinely appreciate the invite. You've made my day!"

Caron smiled. "Glad I could help stroke that ego."

They laughed, and Caron began the stacking of potatoes.

At least I have practiced asking, she thought.

She would get braver and ask another coworker. After all, her place was sparkling!

23

CHAPTER 8

Later that evening, feeling like nothing was really holding her back, Caron took the leap and made the call to the number on the flyer. The number was answered by a man who asked first for the letters below the phone number from the flyer, then he asked preliminary questions about her background and motives for her interest in the position.

The man explained it was a private security-protection company whose focus was to proactively thwart threats to important people like celebrities, politicians, or wealthy persons in general. The job would be ever changing with varying assignments to be fully explained to the employee on a need-to-know basis.

There would be intensive training for about six months to a year to prepare for the position, and there would be no outside contact with family or friends during that first year until completion.

If Caron believed she could meet those basic requirements, she should report to their offices at the corner of Wabash and Patterson Avenues in Baltimore by 7:00 a.m. the next day.

At the conclusion of the training period, all recruits were to receive $50,000 whether or not they met the program requirements. If she were uncertain and needed additional time to discuss this with her family, that would be fine. The next class would begin in six months, and she would be welcome to join then.

Caron felt a bit nervous and pressured as she hung up the phone. This sounded very intense but then again super exciting. Could she just up and go? Could she quit without giving a two weeks' notice to work? Certainly six months would not be so tough to wait and think this through.

Caron grabbed her hoodie and headed back out for the gym. She wanted to run this opportunity by Mike. She felt certain he would provide clarity and help her with the decision. The offer was very rushed, and she was feeling pressure to make the decision too quickly. But it also felt extremely exciting, and she needed something to be excited about in her life.

CHAPTER 9

Reggie greeted her with a quizzical look and said, "Aren't you a bit early today?"

Caron smiled and responded, "I missed your ugly face," and Reggie laughed loudly.

She headed back to Mike's area of the gym and watched while he finished up hand-to-hand training with a young man.

"What brings you here so early today?" asked Mike.

Caron responded, "I need honest advice on a career opportunity I found. I called the number from this flyer for security positions. They want me to come in tomorrow morning."

Caron explained the conversation, and the commitment involved for this potential, new job.

Mike's response was not at all expected. He was downright excited.

"This is fantastic! You would be so completely perfect for a position like this. You are trained and confident already. You will excel through that program and be out working for a client in no time. I am so happy for you, Caron!"

"So I'm surmising you think I should take this job, huh?" Caron replied, smiling.

"Absolutely!" said Mike. "What reservations do you have?"

"I suppose none really. Except the right thing to do would be to give notice at the grocery store." Caron frowned as she said this. *The Shopper's Market has mostly been good to me*, she thought.

Mike shot back, "And miss an opportunity like this? Who knows, they may not have another class for some reason for another year."

And with that point made, Caron nodded. She now knew she was going to do this. In her heart she knew the answer, even before she consulted Mike.

Caron, the bodyguard. She laughed to herself. *Caron the threat thwarter. Yep. That is me, able to leap tall buildings in a single bound! Okay maybe not, but I am excited to find a new career.*

"I got this," she whispered out loud.

CHAPTER 10

Caron walked with a noticeable spring in her step as she passed the row of checkout lanes on her way to the front office. The manager was leaning over and counting money quickly, and Caron waited for him to finish his stack of tens.

"Hi, Sam. I wanted to let you know I will not be back tomorrow. I apologize for not giving you notice, but my new employer wants me to start tomorrow morning." Caron handed up an apron to the stunned store manager.

Seeing his mouth drop open, Caron turned and walked back toward the produce department to say goodbye to Eddie.

Eddie, too, was stunned.

"Just like that? You up and leave just like that? No nothing?" he asked.

Caron laughed and told him about the opportunity and that she was excited and did not want to wait six more months to get started. She hugged Eddie and thanked him for his friendship then headed for the door.

It felt liberating to be done with the store on some level.

Not dealing with customer complaints ever again is the icing on this cake, she thought.

Caron next hit the bank. She did not have much and was able to pull out most of the remaining money, less the rent she intended to pay.

At home, she collected the things important to her—an old novel *Anna Karenina*, some of her clothes, workout gear, and her running shoes. She had not collected a lot of belongings and was not sad to leave things behind.

She left an extra month's rent check on the kitchen table with a note to her property owner stating he may do whatever he wanted with her belongings: sell, donate, whatever. She would not be returning after taking a position that required her to immediately move to a new city. That part was a white lie, but she did not know what else might work that would not require her to pay the entirety of her contract for the year.

She was glad that she had taken the time to clean so thoroughly too, and nobody would see the scratches on the floorboard. She carefully lifted the board one last time to stow her social security card, birth certificate, and the knife with the pearl-looking handle she had taken from Johnny Boy that she had come to love. She figured she would be able to break back into the place in the future if she needed these. For now, the floor would serve as a free bank safety-deposit box.

Caron rummaged through pockets and added the rest of her money, $250. She also took the flyer from her refrigerator and smiled and said, "Why not?" and tossed that in there too. Using Krazy Glue, she carefully secured the board back in place and stood up to admire her handiwork. Now she felt ready to leave this life behind. There would be no sleep for Caron, and she was up and gone from home well ahead of time for her appointment on Patterson Avenue.

CHAPTER 11

Caron waited nervously for her name to be called. Once it was, she jumped up a little too eagerly and saw the motion was not lost on the security guard sitting behind the key-guarded entry gate. He smiled at her, and she nodded and followed him to a small room just inside the door.

The security guard indicated that she should sit in a chair directly across the table from a wiry-looking man with glasses propped on his sweaty head. He appeared to be reading over some notes, and Caron assumed they were from their previous phone conversation.

"Hello, Ms. Tucker," Mr. Sweaty Head began. "I need to begin by saying this conversation is being recorded. My name is Anderson Kent, counsel for Henderson and Associates. I am glad you could make this class on short notice, as the company is in dire need of new assets at this time. It is my job to ensure you understand and agree to the guidelines set as a condition of employment. You will be sequestered, with your group, in a secure location for training for six to twelve months, depending on your progression. Whether or not you pass and are accepted into the program, you must remain until the completion of all training to protect the others in the program as well as the location. Do you understand?"

"Yes," Caron answered.

"You will also be paid $50,000 regardless of your outcome so long as you follow that guideline. Do you understand?"

"Yes," Caron replied once more.

With the parameters agreed upon, Anderson extended his hand to shake and said in a monotoned voice, "Welcome aboard. Do you have any questions?" Caron indicated that she did not, and he handed her a slip of paper with an address and said, "Proceed to this address immediately please."

Caron stood and thanked him and left the office.

The security guard again let her through the key-carded gate, and she exited back onto the street to begin her walk to the next location. She pulled out her phone and punched in the address to quickly get on her way. Pure adrenaline was propelling her at this point, and she was walking so fast that she was almost at a run.

CHAPTER 12

"Welcome to Henderson and Associates. There are two trash cans outside to the right. Use them. Now," a very tall woman with jet-black hair and steely-gray eyes issued the order.

She appeared to be made of one solid muscle on top of another. Daunting for sure. At her feet lay a canvas satchel that looked empty. The recruits looked at one another, not knowing what the instructor meant exactly.

Three women and two men were standing in a small, unassuming house on Ferndale Avenue in an old section of Northwest Baltimore, where they were told to report. It was not terribly far from the recruitment center.

The first floor had been gutted, padded, and made into a gym of sorts. The windows were barred and blackened with dark shades. There was a myriad of weapons ranging from small knives to automatic and sniper-style rifles hanging on the far wall at the back and ropes, tape, zip ties, handcuffs, and other things used to restrain to the left of those. Right underneath on the same wall sat a stack of free weights and two weight benches.

Chairs were stacked high in a corner behind the group next to the front door. In the opposite corner, there were boxes, each labeled with a recruit's name. Caron noticed hers was exactly in the middle. The ceiling light fixtures were wrapped in cages to protect the light bulbs.

To her right was a set of narrow steps leading up. And just below those was a door, which probably were the steps down to the basement. There was something on the other side of the steps, perhaps a bathroom, but she could not see around the corner.

The instructor barked again, "If you plan to work for us, you each must cease to exist and assume new appointed identities. A ghost if you will. Whatever you brought with you must now go in the trash—everything you brought with you right down to your underwear.

"You should have noticed the box with your name on it by now. If you have not, this is not the job opportunity for you. Open your box and consider your training to have begun. There will be no turning back.

"If you fail in this program at any point, you will be put up in a secured location until the rest of the recruits have completed their training. This is a covert location that cannot run the risk of detection should you or I decide this is not right for you. Get your box and change into the clothes provided immediately and deposit your old identity in the trash. Do not make me request this or anything twice."

Caron turned to get her box. As Joe was pulling his box off the top, he asked where he should change.

The instructor had an incredulous look on her face as she said, "Please go around the steps and talk to Mr. Smith. Your services are no longer required."

Shelly, owner of the next box down in the stack, shot a nervous glance at Caron as she lifted hers off. Caron was next, followed by Antoine, then Suzanne. The recruits quickly changed their clothes without a word and dumped all their old belongings into the trash cans as requested.

Having to throw away her well-worn copy of *Anna Karenina* hurt. Caron had found it lying on the sidewalk one day when she was twelve and picked it up because the title was similar to her name. She had read it many times over the years and knew the story well. It had been her escape through the years, her best friend.

The recruits returned to the house to hear Joe's pleas to the mysterious Mr. Smith go unanswered. And just like that, they were down to four recruits. Once the remaining four were in the plain black sweats provided, the instructor proceeded.

"Hello, recruits. My name is Helga. I am your advisor, and I will get you up to date with the program and our requirements. My name was not always Helga, but eventually I thought it fitting by the time I completed my first year of training. We have reidentified you all, and this will be your first step toward becoming an asset."

Helga reached into the seemingly empty satchel and pulled out identification packets for each student. Antoine became Marcus Jones. Shelly became Allison Kincaid. Suzanne became Dakota Gibson. And Caron became Jackie Ford.

"Your first assignment is to learn your new identity. You must know all the details provided in your folder, and supply the information on demand. Read, reread, and then do it again. Live and breathe the details because your life could depend on this at some point, and to hesitate might mean your death.

"I want to emphasize that your previous life no longer exists. We hope you understand that we require this for the protection of your families." Helga picked up her satchel and pointed toward the stairs going up. "Please find your sleeping quarters and settle in quietly to study. Lunch will be served at noon. Dinner at 5:00 p.m."

CHAPTER 13

Caron, now Jackie, settled into the corner bed of the dorm-style room and opened her file. She was no longer from Baltimore, she read, feeling no love lost. Now she was from a small town in upstate New York called Painted Post, just outside of Corning in the Finger Lakes region.

Painted Post is a town whose name was derived from a post that the Seneca Indians used to exchange messages, or it was a post that marked the grave of a great Indian chief, depending on who told the story. When White settlers moved in and pushed out the Native Americans, they painted the post.

Jackie was raised by a grandmother who died when she was eighteen. Grandmother's old abandoned farm still sits on Meads Creek Road, empty and overgrown. As Caron read on and on, she decided Jackie's childhood was fun—frequent trips to Kueka Lake for kayaking or fishing off the family boat, swimming in Meads Creek during the summer months or following it for miles when it dried up in the fall, collecting fossils that should not have been present. There was riding ATVs down the county pipeline and mudding in the pits at the bottom and bonfires and cow tipping after dark.

Jackie's activities were outside, far different from her city life as the daughter of drug addicts. She liked her new identity and embraced it wholeheartedly. She thought she would enjoy going to see the area some day in the future.

At lunch, Helga had everyone introduce themselves and state a favorite childhood memory. This was not in her file, so Jackie had to invent a memory on the spot.

She smiled and spoke of Painted Post and the time she took a four-wheeler up the back hill along the pipeline with a friend. When they got to the other side of the hill, there was a big mud pit. They mudded until they were completely covered, and their machines were choking.

When they got back home, Grandma was furious. Jackie not only had to wash down the four-wheeler but also the whole kitchen, where she had tracked in the mud.

"For the rest of the summer, Grandma would say, 'Your name is Mud,'" Jackie said as she laughed.

Helga nodded approval. "Not bad," she said. "Now work on getting rid of the Baltimore accent and adopting the nasally New York one."

Helga continued with the other three trainees and critiqued their stories as she had Jackie's, reminding them that all situations may not be covered in a file and they would need to be quick on their feet.

Day one was easy thought the recruits as they lay talking in bed that night, comparing experiences. Marcus was strong from his weightlifting competitions. According to him, he was a champion in dead lifts and squats.

Allison was a local gym boxer, who was quiet and offered no backstory, though she seemed very attentive to all the chatter.

Dakota had learned skills in the army. She chose the military life to escape an abusive crackhead mother.

Jackie shared her quest for strength and self-defense cautiously. She knew nobody before truly believed the number of attacks she'd survived in her short life, so she only spoke of the first incident as her motivation to first learn self-defense and then now, to join the agency.

Jackie thought she saw Allison react with a shudder as she revealed the limited details of that first assault. Still, Allison remained stoic and chose to say nothing of her past.

CHAPTER 14

Day two started at 6:00 a.m. Helga herded the recruits out the door for a six-mile run before breakfast.

"You will head right once you are outside and run straight until you reach Liberty Heights Avenue. There, you will turn left and run until you arrive at Mondawmin Mall, which is three miles. Once there, you will continue your run around the perimeter road of the mall and head back the way you came. Today, I am feeling generous, so you have fifty minutes to complete this task."

The audible click of Helga's stopwatch signaled their start, and they began their journey. Marcus shot out quickly, and the rest of them quickly lost sight of him. The women hung together and ran at an easy, steady pace and soon reached the turnaround. Jackie was happy that she was a runner before she accepted this position but held that emotion inside.

As they headed back to the little house on Ferndale Avenue, they encountered Marcus leaning against a stone wall resting. His bulky frame was not conducive to the fast start or a long run. It was not looking good for Marcus. The women returned in forty-eight minutes and watched Helga lock the door at fifty minutes. A few minutes later, they heard Marcus being told to speak with Mr. Smith. It appeared that Marcus, too, was done with the training.

After a hearty breakfast of eggs, grits and sausage, the women were introduced to Bucky to begin their weight training. Bucky was the epitome of a man with that name. Worn blue jeans and a blue plaid flannel shirt decorated his body. He was muscly and of average height with unruly light-brown hair. He was just missing the cowboy boots and hat to complete the look. Caron was sure he was made to remove them for training.

Bucky instructed the recruits on basic weightlifting safety, reiterating that he would be held accountable should a recruit become injured. They took turns doing repetitions as instructed until it was time for lunch. Day one of lifting turned out to be easy for all three women.

Lunch was surprisingly delicious for Caron. She had never tried salmon before but found that she loved it. In fact, she devoured the salmon along with the salad it had rested on. She looked up and realized the others were still picking at their food and felt embarrassed for a moment. But only for a moment.

Next up on the day's agenda was hand-to-hand and weapon training with Carlos. Caron realized she had an issue with stereotyping when Carlos stood before her. She expected an average-sized Latino man, but clearly Carlos was Black. He so closely resembled the man who played the part of Ghost on the show *Power* that she found herself staring and wondering if it was really him.

Carlos began with break-away scenarios. They each took turns getting out of Carlos's holds as instructed. He did not go light on the women and left a few bruised hand-print marks on their arms, necks, and legs.

When 5:00 p.m. arrived, it was time for dinner. Carlos released the women with the instruction that sessions would become more intense over the weeks and that they needed to get as much rest as possible.

Dinner was packed with nutrition, meant to fuel their hardworking bodies. They were served quinoa bowls with an abundance of chicken, spinach, cranberries, and almonds. Once they finished eating, it was time to stretch.

At 6:00–7:00 p.m., they stretched every conceivable muscle under Bucky's guidance. They concluded stretching and headed for the showers, which signaled the end of the physical day. Grateful to get a moment to rest. They would read and study information provided until lights went dark for sleep at 9:00 p.m. Exhausted, none of the recruits had trouble falling right to sleep.

And so it continued with training, very rigorous and tightly scheduled for the coming months. Increased speed in running and speed in disarmament goals were presented daily. Adeptness and quickness with small weapons like knives and picks were noted in their files.

There were constant questions pulled from their profiles and surprise questions designed to throw them off-balance. The women were focused and intent on succeeding, but mistakes happened from time to time.

Helga clicked her tongue whenever that happened as an acknowledgment that they had failed a task. It became amazing to Jackie how much she dreaded hearing that click of Helga's tongue.

CHAPTER 15

Suddenly, it was the end of month two. At least it felt sudden to the women, as their time seemed to pass very quickly. Training became more in-depth and later involved firearms and interrogation methods.

As they gathered that spring morning, Helga was already seated and looking at a paper and said, "Suzanne, please come here and answer this question."

Suzanne/Dakota approached the table.

Helga then said, "Why are you, after two months, answering to the name Suzanne?"

Stunned, Suzanne lowered her head as Helga said the fateful words, "Your services are no longer required. Please speak with Mr. Smith."

And now, they were just two: Jackie and Allison.

Jackie and Allison stared at each other in a silent vow: they would have to have each other's back. Later at bedtime, they voiced this as an assurance. Jackie believed they were very well matched ability-wise.

Mike's training had provided an excellent base for her, and Allison's boxing had served her well to prepare them for this profession. They were each assigned a new trainer, who would replace Helga going forward.

Allison was paired with a redheaded, freckly young man named Henry. And ironically Jackie was paired with a stocky older Italian-looking man named Mike.

Jackie smiled a moment, recalling her Mike's enthusiasm for this new job. He would be so happy with her right about now. She wished she could share her success to date, but of course, that was out of the question.

The trainers liked to work in unison. Frequently, the women would be side by side doing sit-ups or push-ups. They would take turns on the chin-up bar with their only rest in between sets being while the other was completing their turn.

Jackie lagged behind Allison with the pull-ups, as Allison clearly had more upper-body strength. They would lay side by side on the weight benches, too, and it seemed every few days, more weights were added.

"These trainers have worked us harder than Reggie or Mike ever had me do," Jackie told Allison as they ended yet another exhausting day with a hot shower. "Get a load of these biceps," said Jackie to Allison that evening. "I'm catching up to you."

"We are getting seriously strong," Allison responded. "This workout is no joke. I'm loving my back muscles now."

The women compared more of their body improvements, then headed down to dinner. They both were enjoying this part of training, and they looked forward to the next day.

CHAPTER 16

Shelly

Shelly Carson was happy-go-lucky as a young girl, beautiful and bright. At least that was what her foster father would say to the caseworker whenever he made a home visit. Shelly had been living there since she was seven years old, this being her fifth foster home after being given up by a drug addict of a mother.

Father Tony started out with strict rules initially. Her life was structured in perfect neatness right down to her underwear drawer. Inspections were daily, and rarely did she escape a beating for something trivial like a shoelace touching the floor.

"But something got into her in her teens, and she's been difficult since," Father Tony continued.

Mr. Benson, the caseworker in charge of this unplanned visit, nodded.

Mr. Benson heard that scenario countless times he thought as he checked off the necessary boxes and finished his report. Shelly sat quietly during the visit, as she knew better if she wanted to avoid any extra punishment.

Father Tony, as he made her call him, was harsh to put it simply. There was one time when Shelly spoke up to the caseworker. Father Tony easily talked away her claims, saying, "She isn't happy with her curfew." As soon as Mr. Benson left, she felt his punch hit the back of her head. She fell to the floor only to be kicked repeatedly then dragged by her hair to the basement vault.

The vault was a concrete room at the back of the basement with a heavy door and lock and with no window and no escape. Shelly had seen that room so many times she started to sneak things down there for comfort ahead of the inevitable punishment.

But that day, she barely moved a sore muscle as the caseworker continued through his questions. Shelly answered that she was contented living here.

She hid the fact that just the night before this surprise social worker visit, Father Tony had locked her in the vault with two men who abused her body and raped her repeatedly through the night. Shelly had just gotten out of a shower and dressed when the doorbell chimed. If only he had arrived an hour earlier. She might have been freed from this monster.

But in truth, Shelly knew she would never have that kind of good luck. As she sat there through the caseworker's interview, Shelly thought she portrayed a happy sixteen-year-old to the caseworker, but apparently, it was not enough to satisfy Father Tony.

As soon as Child Protective Services left, his anger was spitting out of his mouth as he ordered Shelly to take off all her clothes. She knew he was going to make her get in one of the ice baths he had forced on her in the past.

Father Tony began to run the cold water in the bathtub, got the ice bin from the freezer, and dumped in its contents. These last few punishments had gotten her toughened up to face Father Tony and defy his request.

He may be strong and fit, but so am I, she thought.

No, she would not willingly disrobe and get in an ice bath. This needed to stop, and she said as much to the irate, red-faced monster standing before her.

Father Tony punched Shelly so hard in the stomach she lost her wind. He slugged her in her face and ripped the buttons off her blouse as he tore it off her and demanded she comply. Once again, she acquiesced. But she knew this would be the last.

To date, Shelly had endured nine years of Father Tony's abuse. So, at 3:00 a.m., Shelly dumped out the school contents of her backpack and stuffed in a couple of changes of clothes and some toiletries.

She braided her long blonde hair and tucked it up with a hat. Her green eyes were still striking despite the bruises that were taking over. She did not bother with a concealer this time.

Fuck it, she thought as she crept out of the bedroom. *And fuck you, too, Father Tony.*

She resisted the urge to slam the door as she left, thinking he would be quick to catch her. But still, she took off at a run just in case he did hear something.

For the rest of the night, she would sleep with the homeless behind the library of her small town. She thought she might miss Westminster and the good people she cared for there, but Shelly knew she needed to move on.

She decided to head to Owings Mills in the morning, walking all back roads to get there. Feeling free, she slept without fear for the first time in nine years.

CHAPTER 17

The Metro Centre at Owings Mills was Shelly's resting point. She had made it there quicker than she expected and would have the rest of the day to decide what to do next.

She found a Starbucks coffee shop and ducked inside to use the restroom. On her way out, she saw a community board and read all the attached notices hoping for an under-the-table sort of job but had no luck.

Shelly decided to hop on the metro and head down to Baltimore to get lost in the people. Surely Father Tony would not think to look there. At least not yet.

Shelly sank into a seat and quickly fell asleep. The exhaustion of the long walk as well the previous day's events both plagued her. She awoke to the end-of-the-line message over the speaker and another passenger shaking her awake.

As she exited the station, she looked up high at the buildings surrounding her.

This day is the first day of my future, she thought with feigned bravery.

There would be no more beatings and no more men to rape her.

She decided to walk west, and within a few blocks, she came to a boxing gym. Feeling like it was fate, she walked in.

James greeted her with a "Lookee here, we got some youngin' peeking in on our fine ee-stablishment."

Shelly could not resist and laughed a little too loud.

"What can we do for you?" James asked.

James was just an average-looking man of about sixty with very light-black skin. He was tall and had a warm smile and kind eyes. Not what you would expect when you walk into a boxing gym.

"I'd like to take lessons, please. How do I go about that?" Shelly replied.

Now it was James's turn to laugh loudly. "Child, you would be eaten alive in here. Now go get on your way."

Shelly teared up and said in a quivering voice, "You don't understand. I need to learn to protect myself. I must. It's my only priority right now."

"Why here?" he asked.

"Because Father Tony would never look here for me," she replied.

James's laughter quickly turned to concern.

"Who is Father Tony, and why are you hiding from him?" he asked.

Shelly realized she blurted out more than she should have and did not know the right way to respond.

"Someone I never want to see again, and if I do, I want to be prepared."

James nodded, clearly troubled. He had seen other troubled kids from his West Baltimore neighborhood in the past and had discreetly helped them. His gut said this one was desperate.

"Come on in. Let's see what we can do for you."

James guided her to the back office and invited her to sit.

Shelly began by saying, "I don't have a lot of money, but I could do work as a trade if you'll let me."

James responded, "Perhaps that can be arranged. I assume you need a place to sleep?"

Shelly's eyes widened. "How do you know that?"

There was something about James that made Shelly feel safe. She looked into his kind black eyes and offered her sincere gratitude.

James thought, *This young girl has been abused. Lord help that Father Tony if he should ever step in this place looking for her.*

She looked to be about sixteen, he estimated. James had no patience for a man who abused women or children. None at all.

CHAPTER 18

Shelly soon became the resident boxer girl and easily fit right in. Her personality was sweet, and she always looked to please. James thought the gym had never looked so good ever since Shelly organized and cleaned and kept it up in general.

Shelly also thrived under the direction of Gerald, her coach, and learned to deftly avoid hits or takedowns. She worked hard and gained great strength, particularly in her arms. She marveled at her biceps one day in a little mirror and smiled. She had come so far in a brief period. She also began to open up to James about her past.

*****

James had slowly been asking her questions to gain insight on his little bird who lost her nest. He liked to call her Little Bird affectionately. Shelly knew he was working to understand her situation and finally told him her ugly truths one evening after dinner.

Shelly felt vindicated by James's reaction, as clearly the man was filling with anger right before her eyes. Finally someone believed her. It was a relief, and in truth, it was enough for Shelly.

James wanted Father Tony's address, but Shelly would not give it up. The last thing she wanted was for James to go to jail after he had been such a caring man and taking her in. James breathed life back into Shelly; she would not be a part of having his stolen.

When Shelly was not training, she mostly hid out in the back room but would venture out to get food when the little refrigerator in her room got bare. On one such venture, she looked at the community board, as she always did, and found a leaflet with tear-off numbers at the bottom. It read:

CAREER IN DEFENSE

Are you looking for an exciting career in defense?

We offer paid training to the right candidates.

We will train and supply you everything necessary for the position.

Women are strongly encouraged to apply.

Must be willing to travel.

Call for more information.

Shelly tore off the number and headed back to the gym.

Maybe this job opportunity would be a good thing for her to investigate. She could not live in the back of the gym forever now that she was eighteen.

James had become a father to her, so it was natural that she would want to get his opinion on this new opportunity. He was excited when Shelly told him of the notice.

"Let's call and get the details. Who knows? This could be such an adventurous job for you. God knows you have the fire in your belly to succeed at something like this."

Together, they called, and the details proved to be quite enticing. James had such confidence in Shelly succeeding that she did not have any doubts herself. She would apply for this job, and she would get hired, and she would do well. She knew it in her soul.

The company spokesperson said the next class would be beginning a week from Monday, so Shelly had a little time to say her goodbyes to everyone. She made her way around the gym, but there was one last thing she really needed to do. She asked James to take her to Father Tony's house.

James accompanied her to the door, and when Father Tony looked out of the window, he refused to open the door. Shelly shook her head and produced the old key from her purse and opened the door herself.

Father Tony did not have enough time to stand from his chair and escape Shelly's punch to his nose. The crack it made as it broke was extremely satisfying to her. She ordered Father Tony to sit in his chair while she went into the basement and searched the vault to ensure no other little girl was within it.

Shelly continued to search the entire house and was satisfied that Father Tony was living alone. When she returned to the living room, James was still leering angrily at Father Tony. She confirmed the absence of any other children.

Shelly then returned her attention to Father Tony and said, "Take your clothes off."

Father Tony started to protest, but James inched slightly closer and provided the perfect amount of intimidation.

Shelly started the bathwater and retrieved the ice from the freezer. She heard James say in hushed voice, "You are lucky to be alive after Shelly told me what you did. If I had my way… Hell, I may have to come back and have my way later."

He quieted as Shelly returned to the room and ordered Father Tony into the tub.

This part, she had to admit, was not nearly as satisfying, but there was some finality to it all, like having the last word after a vicious argument and knowing there was nothing the other person could say to top you.

CHAPTER 19

Shelly was a bit melancholy but also excited as she headed to report to this new job. The last year and a half with James at the gym was truly healing. She had met some good people and learned to love and trust again.

Shelly also had never felt so loved before this and knew she would miss James sorely. Promising to keep in touch when she could was all she had to offer James back.

She rang the gym bell for the last time and headed out into the cold autumn morning. Shelly figured that walking to the Patterson Avenue office would be cleansing for her despite the chill from the breeze.

As she anticipated, Shelly was hired. She had a brief vetting process where she agreed to their terms of committing to finishing the program. She walked to the little house on Ferndale Avenue as instructed and began her career for Henderson and Associates.

CHAPTER 20

Month three arrived without either of the women realizing how much time had passed. One frigid winter morning, Jackie and Allison were invited to sit at the table and were presented with pistols.

Mike, obviously the senior instructor, began. "You will learn this firearm inside and out. You will disassemble, clean, reassemble. Once you are confident you can do this without instruction, we will proceed to the next step."

Henry demonstrated on a Springfield XD. He deftly disassembled and reassembled the small gun and asked if they had questions. Shaking no, both instructors disappeared around the corner toward Mr. Smith.

As luck would have it, this was one of the guns that Old Mike, the Navy SEAL, had trained Jackie on. She quickly completed her assignment and discreetly helped Allison do the same.

They took apart, cleaned, and reassembled the gun for a few hours, knowing they were being watched. The instructors reappeared and asked if they were confident in their ability to complete this task.

They replied in unison, "Yes."

Each recruit was fitted with a blindfold, and the task was again requested. Each completed the task perfectly.

They were then escorted to the basement where a firing range had been installed. It appeared to be mostly underground, and Jackie thought, *They must have tunneled underground toward the back of the house to make this happen.* It did not fit with the above-grade part of the house where they had lived the past couple of months.

There were two range lanes with stands near the front side. On each stand lay a set of ears and eyes protection for each of them. They were instructed to put them on and told how to use the target line. Spare targets were below the stand to replenish as needed.

They were shown stance and grips, which they were to practice over the next four hours. Mike and Henry were nearby, coaching them along on their stance, patience, reaction, and accuracy as they practiced.

Jackie was secretly pleased to see Allison progress so quickly with this assignment. She had been through this quite thoroughly with Old Mike and felt confident in this arena.

She heard Mike say they were naturals, as he hauled in another target with the bull's-eye shot out, and this was the only time during the duration of training that he would exhibit a smile.

Next they moved on to shotguns and rifles with the same intensive practice then automatic rifles then long-range sniper rifles. They managed to fire every weapon hanging on that back wall, and by the end of month three, they were both deemed experts by both Mike and Henry. The instructors indicated a report would be sent up to Helga stating this.

By their fourth month, each day had a pattern of early morning runs then weights then drills with every aspect of every weapon until they dropped from exhaustion. There was a parade of assets who tested with them to allow for imagination of attack and response. Every conceivable scenario presented, they conquered.

Helga received daily updates and was pleased with the speed of their progression through the program. Within six months, they both were declared as having completed the training program and ready for assignment.

Helga selected two files from her bin of urgent assignments. The newest assets were indeed proving to be the best to date to come out of the program. She would give them their first test. She turned out the lights and closed her office for the evening.

CHAPTER 21

Jackie and Allison received the news of their acceptable completion of training and admitted to each other that they were excited for their first appointments. They realized it could not be a huge assignment, but it would be their start.

Helga appeared and looked genuinely pleased with the progress reports she waved at the recruits. She called Jackie up first and handed her a file.

"This is completely confidential to you. No one else, including Allison, including Mike, and including Henry. All your future assignments will also be handed to you with this confidentiality criteria. I am sure you fully understand the necessity by now."

Jackie spoke her understanding, took the file, and retreated backward.

Helga called up Allison and gave her a file also with the same instructions. She then dismissed them both to begin their career as protection assets for Henderson and Associates.

*****

Jackie sat on the bed in the dorm room to view her assignment and see where this journey was to take her. The paperwork started with a briefing page. On it was the pertinent information as a summary:

Car—silver Mercedes sedan

MD tag 1DF4677, door PIN 3810, keys under driver's seat

Phone—locked in glove box, PIN 3810 ID, and credit cards—also in glove box.

You will keep these until further instructions are received.

Hotel—Hilton Baltimore. Open app on your phone for the room number and door key

Clothing—All you need for this assignment will be in your hotel room.

Subject—John Hansen, CEO of Hansen Aerospace IT

On the second page, there was a summary of who John Hansen was and his requests. He was a self-made billionaire selling IT software to aerospace companies.

He recently had a young man come forward who claimed to be his son. He is not. That man's name is Seth Ryan (pictures included).

Ryan has made death threats and warned of exposing Hansen in the public if he is not compensated. Ryan is not to be taken lightly. He has a history of violence and was recently released from jail (full criminal file included).

Hansen has requested a female bodyguard to escort him to an conference in Seattle, Washington, for a couple of days.

There, you will act as his date. You will protect Hansen from Seth Ryan should he be present and are authorized to use deadly force if necessary.

Jackie opened the files and studied the pictures of a twenty-something man with jet-black hair and eyes. He was tallish at six feet and one inch and soft. Most of his pictures were in jeans and sweat-shirts, so Jackie imagined him in a suit as well.

She etched his face in her mind then turned to the criminal file. Drugs seemed to be at the center of his incarcerations. He robbed a couple of stores but really got his jail time for an assault on a man who did not give up his wallet on command.

Ryan does not seem extraordinarily violent, but you never know, she thought.

Jackie grabbed her toiletries and headed out, stopping to wish Allison good luck on her way. Allison gave her a thumbs-up and smiled. Jackie easily found the Mercedes outside the front door and then drove directly to the Hilton.

CHAPTER 22

Allison retreated to her room as well and read her file from Helga. She too found the summary page of her assignment.

> Car—black Chevy Suburban MD tag 7DC0112, door PIN 6679, keys under driver's seat
>
> Phone—locked in glove box, PIN 6679 ID, and credit cards—also in glove box. You will keep these until further instruction is given.
>
> Hotel—Hilton Chesapeake, VA. Open app on your phone for the room number and door key.
>
> Clothing—All needed for this assignment will be in your hotel room.
>
> Subject—Ellee Moreno, rap star
>
> Ellee Moreno is a rap music artist who recently was entangled in a love triangle. The other two participants of the triangle are Milanya Roberts and Kelvin Smith (pictures enclosed). Smith did not inform Roberts he was also seeing Moreno.
>
> Roberts has confronted Moreno numerous times and more recently issued death threats. Moreno has requested a female bodyguard to escort her to performances while she is working in the

Hampton Roads area. Deadly force is permitted should you find it necessary.

Additional information on Milanya Roberts— age 28, 5'5", 150 lbs. Wears wigs and frequently changes her appearance. Criminal record (see file included) shows history of violence to other women with some jail time.

Kelvin Smith—age 32, 5'10", 175 lbs. Criminal record—none found.

The shit is real, thought Allison as she, too, gathered up her toiletries and exited the house that she had lived in for the past six months. Allison looked back at the house as she exited.

There is no way anyone would suspect what is going on in there, she thought.

She hopped in the Suburban and headed south.

CHAPTER 23

Jack Franklin was a formidable man at 6'5" and 325 lbs. His hair was mostly dark but showed signs of graying around his temples. He had deep dimples which he used thoroughly to his advantage when he smiled to charm people. His pale complexion did little to hide the scar that ran across his right cheek. The scar was inherited from his mother when he was a teenager and served as a constant reminder of why he hated women.

Mother's abuse was severe and lasted long until one day, Jack simply killed her. He then deposited her body in a smelly trash dumpster behind his apartment.

Nobody was ever the wiser because Jack had taught himself how to cleverly go from one personality to another to suit the situation in front of him. He was deeply troubled as he called the police when it became apparent his mother was not returning home. It had been four days, and his concern was plainly visible on his face as he made the report to the young cop who responded to his call.

Jack was just seventeen years old when his mother went missing. He was just shy of being able to go free on his own and was sent to a halfway house.

The arrangement was not satisfactory for Jack, and he decided to convince the court of a better option for his care. He requested consent be given for him to join the Navy, and the court eagerly granted this.

Jack excelled in the Navy and rose through the ranks very quickly to master chief. He used his skills of charm to endear people along the way while working hard as a sailor.

It did not come as a surprise to Jack that the commander of his unit took notice and summoned him to his office one day. Jack had been manipulating the commander from the moment they met.

Commander Kane wanted to groom Jack for a position outside of the military but government-sponsored doing covert missions. Jack appeared to excel at everything to Kane, including following orders, which would be pivotal in the new role once Jack's fourth tour of duty was finished.

"This new opportunity would be all-consuming and, at times, quite lonely," explained Commander Kane.

This was not a deterrent to Jack because it fit with his personality. Jack enjoyed his own company above all others and had never felt lonely before in his life. He did not suffer fools well and felt most people were exactly that in his eyes: damn fools.

Jack accepted with feigned gratitude and soon joined the company, Henderson and Associates. Henderson and Associates was well hidden in multiple layers of the government.

On the surface, Henderson was known as a company that provided security to VIPs. Below its surface and within those layers were the government-sanctioned assassins.

The new role suited him perfectly; he got paid to kill people. In Jack's eyes, nothing could be better than the freedom and compensation this role afforded him.

A dozen years later and after an exemplary record, Commander Kane appointed him as principal of Henderson and Associates. Commander Kane taught Jack everything he needed to learn to continue with both sides of the company programs.

Jack had innovative ideas too. He was a man with an inflated ego and felt he could dominate and intimidate people into complying with whatever he desired. He was determined to lead the covert program into a new era.

One of his ideas was to build an elite army of female assassins as a covert program within the covert program. This was where and how the Franklin Project was born.

Many people in the organization balked at what Jack was proposing to do, but he refused to listen. Instead he released anyone who dared to contradict him in any way. Jack eventually found the right people to execute his project and started putting it in place in early 1990.

CHAPTER 24

"The two newest subjects are superb," Helga reported to Jack as she neatly folded herself into a chair. "They have completed the six months training program and have been given their first assignments. Here are their files."

Jack took the files and scanned to see which girls came on board and was pleased to see Caron Tucker's name. She was one of six in the accelerated program, and he knew she had to be tough to have survived. Most subjects had already committed suicide.

Caron had cost a lot of money to develop. He was sincerely glad she was not yet another terminated girl. He also loved the irony of her name being Jackie now. It made him feel like she was his personal creation.

Shelly Carson was a little different. It did not take as much money to pay for her cultivation, and it was not the same level, but hey, here she was too.

Excellent, he thought. "Keep me updated" was all Jack said and waved Helga away.

Jack liked Helga despite her being a woman. She was nasty and edgy and hated women too. If she were better to look at, he might have considered more with her.

But Helga was extremely competent, another attribute he did not usually associate with women. He watched her walk away and thought she looked like a man from behind.

What a shame, he thought.

Jack's sexual tastes were squarely in line with his personality. He occasionally frequented a BDSM (Bondage, Discipline, Sadism, Masochism) club in an old warehouse in southwest Baltimore. It was there he would take of his violent urges and try to regain self-control.

At the club, he could outwardly abuse women undetected, and he liked to be seen doing this. Jack went undetected because many women enjoyed being beaten up and bruised, which fit perfectly with what he preferred.

Jack would bring a suitcase filled with his collection of instruments designed to inflict pain. He usually alternated between a riding crop and a belt with a big square buckle for his beatings.

Jack would inevitably find one of his regulars when he stopped in and would restrain her to a Saint Andrew's cross or whatever apparatus was available. He would then begin beating her ass until it turned a bright red then purple. Several times, he had drawn blood, and that only further excited him. He would then fuck her hard while bystanders watched until he was done with his brutal assault and some of his anger inside was appeased.

*****

Many of the patrons were wary of this man known as the Dom Damian. He was more extreme than most of the patrons and did not seem to be concerned about his partner's safety. A safety monitor once had to rescue a woman bound too tightly to an apparatus. She repeatedly requested that Dom Damian loosen the ties, but he refused. The monitor intervened, and Dom Damian was issued a warning. He would be permanently expelled if this happened again.

Many patrons of the community tried to communicate to Dom Damian that the violence seemed excessive, but he just smiled his knowing smile. People in this club were very in tune usually and engaged in BDSM safely when playing out scenes. But everyone knew it was not evident with this dom. He clearly hid behind the mask and pretended. The women who braved his assault wore it like a badge of honor. They could "take it." And so Dom Damian continued to dish it out severely.

CHAPTER 25

Jackie arrived at the Hilton twenty minutes later and entered her room. She found the clothes as promised as well as a suitcase to put them in. In the bathroom, there was a fresh set of toiletries and makeup. Jackie was not big on makeup but knew that for this role, she would have to figure it out.

There was also very expensive-looking jewelry, and she had to wonder if the diamonds were real. This conference must be fancy considering the gown and jewels. Conveniently, she found a leather firearm strap for her leg to be concealed under her gown. Thankfully the shoes provided had a wide enough heel that she would be able to run in them if necessary.

On the desk, Jackie found first-class tickets on Alaskan Airlines for a direct flight to Seattle. The flight would leave at 7:00 a.m. There would be a car to pick her up at 5:00 a.m. and transport her to BWI Thurgood Marshall Airport.

It was only 2:00 p.m. at this point, so Jackie had time to try on the clothes and makeup. She decided first to try on the gown she would wear.

This is amazing, she thought.

The blue sequined dress with a slit up the side revealed her well-toned thigh. Jackie had never had an opportunity to wear such a dress and felt confident and excited.

The gun strapped to her thigh was nicely concealed. No one would ever suspect of its existence. Jackie enjoyed the feeling that she would be incognito and capable all at once.

She fastened the diamond necklace around her neck and inserted the stud earrings. They enhanced her glamorous look, but she knew she needed to tackle the makeup.

Jackie carefully applied a thin layer of the liquid face foundation and marveled at the evenness of her skin tone.

This is easy, she thought and moved on to the eyeliner.

After a few failed attempts, she decided not to use this for now. Next she applied a brown eye shadow and mascara without issue and finished with a deep-red lipstick.

Having satisfied herself that she could pull off the persona of John Hansen's date, Jackie changed back into street clothes and washed the makeup from her face before heading down to the hotel restaurant for dinner.

CHAPTER 26

The next morning, in the lobby, Jackie saw a man holding an iPad with her name on it. She approached, and the man led her to a waiting limo. He opened the door for Jackie who slid into the rear seat, then he loaded her bag into the trunk. As soon as the door shut, Jackie could not contain a wide smile. Traveling in style was a perk she had not considered before now. She looked around the limo and knew she had made the right decision to join this company.

The limo ride was quick, as there was no traffic, and she soon found herself breezing through the airport to declare her firearm for travel. Everything seemed to proceed smoothly, and she began to wonder how her employer put it all together. She felt like a celebrity because of the ease of security and the offer of a ride to the gate.

Now seated in the very first aisle of first class, Jackie pulled her phone from her bag to check for any communications. None. Helga had reiterated before she departed that she needed to be in touch and answer messages promptly. Her thought process was interrupted by a flight attendant offering a beverage. She accepted coffee with a grateful smile.

Internally Jackie was super excited for the assignment but was trying her best to conceal this. She wondered if Allison was having the same butterflies. She also wondered if she would ever see her again. It was made perfectly clear that they were not to be friends or communicate in any way in the future. If either of the young women needed anything, they were to request this from Helga directly.

The plane landed on the tarmac without issue in Seattle. Jackie exited the airport after collecting her gun and suitcase and once again saw her name on an iPad next to a waiting limo. She settled into the back seat as the driver drove off to meet Mr. John Hansen. This time, she was able to conceal the smile.

As the limo went over the I5 bridge into Seattle, Jackie could see the CenturyLink Field stadium where the Seahawks played. There seemed to be construction cranes everywhere.

The city must be growing, she thought.

She was certain the growth had a lot to do with Amazon and the monster of a company that it had become. They exited the highway and shortly arrived at a restaurant called Il Terrazzo Carmine. Inside was John Hansen who had already ordered their lunch.

CHAPTER 27

John Hansen was a handsome man by everyone's standards with chiseled features and a stately air. His thick blond hair was combed perfectly in place. But the thing about John Hansen that drew you in was his startling blue eyes. They were quite unusual, like clear crystals with a blue backlight. He was clearly a fit man, and it showed in the tailored suit he wore.

John stood to greet Jackie and took her hand in his as they sat down.

"Hello, I'm John Hansen. I'm very pleased you could help me out in this situation."

"My pleasure, Mr. Hansen. I am Jackie Ford. I look forward to working with you."

"You might want to call me John if we are to be dating," he said and winked.

Jackie smiled. "Of course, John."

Throughout an amazing lunch of ravioloni pesce and scaloppine di vitello, John chatted about the conference they were to attend that evening. He gave an in-depth account of the layout of the venue and the times they would be expected at each roundtable discussion. He noted every exit and what was on the other side. Jackie realized John was indeed nervous, worried even.

Did he really expect the faux son to attack him at this conference?

Jackie absorbed this all in and nodded as he continued to deliver every detail that came to mind.

Finally, she interceded. "John, you will be safe with me. I give you my word."

John seemed only a little relieved that Jackie spoke up, but he did stop with the extensive descriptions.

Jackie explained that she would be armed during the evening and that she had extensive training in hand-to-hand combat. She would be fully capable of disarming and subduing any person who would attempt an attack. As they exited the restaurant into a dreary day, John's eyes darted around the street. He was still nervous, Jackie observed.

The limo would drop them both off at the Charter Hotel Seattle where they had adjoining rooms. Once in the room, Jackie shed her clothes for a much-desired bath. She needed a little time to get centered and prepared for her first assignment. She found she was not nervous and was secretly hoping for something to happen so she could prove herself to both John and her company.

Exiting the shower, she pulled a towel around herself and began the process of blow-drying her blond hair that had grown to shoulder-length during her training. Tonight, she would just do a little twist up with her hair and pin it in place. *Elegant*, she thought as she secured the last pin in place. Perhaps she should let her hair stay a little longer, as it allowed for more variety of styles.

After applying the makeup and self approving the job, she strapped her firearm to her thigh. She slipped into the beautiful dress and once again admired her form. With the diamonds added, she felt like a princess, the Disney kind she would dream of as a little girl.

She grabbed her silver clutch and tapped on the adjoining room door to let John know she was ready. John quickly swung the door open as though he was standing there, waiting on her knock.

"Wow," he said with a quick intake of his breath. "I never dreamed I'd get protection in such a beautiful form!"

"Thank you," replied Jackie. "Are you ready?"

"Yes, madam," replied John as he took Jackie's arm and led her from the room.

They were quiet on the way to the convention: John looking over notes for his talks and Jackie imagining scenarios where she would be needed in defense. Neither was talking to the other.

They soon arrived, and the chauffer opened the door for John to exit. John turned and offered a hand to help Jackie out. She took his hand and stepped out onto the sidewalk with the realization that her new job was very real. She would protect this man. A resolve to do just this engulfed her whole body.

Jackie smiled brightly and placed a kiss on John's cheek as she stepped up on the curb. Her eyes scanned the area and noted nothing was out of place. As they entered the building, they were escorted to a cocktail area where many people were currently drinking and laughing or in intimate conversation. Again, nothing out of place.

Jackie realized that John, too, was looking for anything out of the ordinary, but they both came up blank. Things looked perfectly in place. John acknowledged the unspoken words with a nod, and together, they walked over to the bar where John ordered a bourbon on the rocks for himself and a cosmopolitan for Jackie.

Drinks in hand, the two headed to the reception area. John saw his friends from work and introduced Jackie as his friend. They chatted about the upcoming roundtables and where they figured the most could be learned or knowledge imparted.

Jackie played the disinterested girlfriend but kept herself on high alert. She overheard John say to his friends that he knew she would be bored a bit but that she was great fun for later. Jackie did not care. She would never again see this group, so it did not really matter how John explained her away. She could play the part of the dumb blonde for a night.

They mingled more and ate hors d'oeuvres until they were summoned for dinner. John found their seats and pulled a chair for Jackie to sit. Their salads were already presented, as were dinner rolls and bottles of red and white wines.

A robust and cheerful man they had met earlier sat down and bellowed, "Let's all eat, eh?"

The table chuckled, and his wife responded, "We were just waiting for you, Beau."

The table had a lively conversation as dinner of salmon or prime rib was served. It appeared to Jackie that John had visibly relaxed, completely in his element, as he savored the raspberry tart dessert.

Now in need of a restroom, Jackie whispered for him to remain at the table until she returned then excused herself. She hurried herself along, knowing it was never good to have your client out of sight, but some things were unavoidable.

She quickly returned to the table. Everything seemed to be the same. She breathed a sigh of relief. Everyone had finished their dessert and were idly chatting while waiting for the discussions to begin.

The announcement rang out over the intercom for participants to head to the next room for the roundtable sessions. You would have thought there was to be a show or a concert with the level of excitement in the room. People walked quickly to their appointed tables where they immediately began a hushed conversation. John was no different.

Having completely forgotten his worries, he adamantly extolled the virtues of his new radar system. Jackie was to hang with the dates during these conversations and observe from a distance. Had this not been an assignment and an actual date, she would have been quite annoyed at this separation. When the third session ended, John let her know he needed to duck into the bathroom for a minute. Jackie waited nearby, at ease as the night was eventless for her.

John entered the bathroom and used the urinal. As he turned to wash his hands, he heard a stall open and looked up in the mirror and saw the young man, Seth Ryan, in the reflection. Ryan had been patiently waiting for John to come in.

Showing John his gun before tucking it back under his jacket, he motioned for him to leave.

"I will be following right behind you. You will call your car, and we will leave quietly so nobody gets hurts. Do you understand?"

John nodded.

"Pull out your phone and call your car now," Ryan added.

John did as he was told.

"Great. Now let us leave without a ruckus, shall we?"

Ryan pulled the door open and beckoned John out first. He followed closely and propelled John toward the entrance.

Jackie saw the scene unfolding and followed the two outside to the car. Pretending to be the date she was supposed to be, she asked, "I didn't think you wanted to leave already. Don't you have more sessions?"

John replied weakly, "I'm feeling ill, honey. We need to leave now."

"Okay, are we taking a friend too?" Jackie said as she slid into the car next to John.

"Yes," replied Ryan. "We are all going back to the house."

Jackie bided her time, knowing she was better having them out of such close quarters.

"So, darling"—Jackie turned to John—"did the food make you ill? Will we be able to party later?"

John looked at her with quizzical eyes. *What is she thinking?* he thought.

Ryan interjected, "Who are you exactly?"

"Who are you?" replied Jackie sarcastically.

"I'm his son. A son he doesn't like to admit really exists."

Jackie feigned surprised and looked back at John, who was shaking now.

"John, do you really have a son you won't acknowledge? That is dreadful. Why haven't you told me about him? You should be ashamed of yourself and rectify this situation if you intend to have me in your life."

Ryan looked relieved that she was on his side.

"When we get back to the house, you two will sit down and work this out!" Jackie said.

John could not speak. Ryan responded that it was his intent and kept his gun hidden in his jacket pocket.

As they pulled into the circular drive, Ryan's eyes lit up. Jackie was sure it was greed she was seeing. She jumped out of the car first and drew her firearm and put it behind her back. Next out was John, followed quickly by Ryan. Jackie pulled her gun and told Ryan to back away. Instead, he grabbed John and put the gun to his head.

Ryan yelled that she was a liar, too, and that if she did not drop her gun, he would shoot John in the head. Jackie squeezed the trigger without hesitation, and Ryan fell to the ground, shot in the head. John collapsed, too, but unhurt.

John was trembling badly and obviously in shock as Jackie helped him to his feet. The limo driver jumped out and helped get John inside.

Once seated, John looked at Jackie and said, "Thank you. I cannot believe that just happened."

"You are safe now," she responded.

Jackie called into the agency and reported what had transpired. Police were then dispatched and statements taken. The situation was deemed self-defense, as both the chauffeur and John mirrored the details Jackie provided.

Jackie was quite pleased with herself. Her confidence soared, knowing she was able to protect someone so completely. She wanted badly to call Old Mike back at his gym in Baltimore and tell him his training was the real reason she was able to shoot accurately and confidently. But she knew those days were past.

The agency taught her that she had to remain anonymous to be effective in this business. They also taught her that she would immediately be terminated if she were to communicate with her old life. After all she had been through in her life, she wanted to be able to prevent and protect, especially herself.

Jackie's feelings were ones of pride and security and happiness. Maybe it was wrong to feel this way. Maybe she should be upset or sad or despondent over taking someone's life. But she was not despite this being the first time she had killed another person. Instead she was euphoric, and she did not care.

I cannot wait for my next assignment, she thought as she boarded her plane back to Baltimore.

CHAPTER 28

Somewhere over Wyoming, Jackie guessed she must have fallen asleep. She had been on an incredible adrenaline high and crashed. She woke up to the pilot saying they were on their final descent into Baltimore, where the current time was 5:43 p.m. and the temperature was fifty-eight degrees.

Jackie allowed the excitement to return during that final descent then stowed it away once the plane touched down. She retrieved her firearm then her suitcases and called a car to take her back to the Hilton downtown to await further instructions as she was trained to do.

Back in the hotel, Jackie took a quick shower to remove the travel grime and put on some clean clothes. Feeling refreshed and ravenous, she decided to venture out into the inner harbor for some food. It was about 7:00 p.m., and she fully expected to be waiting for a table wherever she went.

Jackie exited the hotel onto Pratt Street and headed toward Light Street. She knew the area and wanted to go to Bubba Gump's for some of her favorite Mama Blues shrimp gumbo. She had not had it in an awfully long time and was looking forward to it.

Waiting in line will not be a problem for me, she thought. *That gumbo is well worth whatever the wait turns out to be.*

At the restaurant, Jackie was pleasantly surprised at the shortness of the line. It was a weeknight, so she guessed that was the reason for the line's brevity. She was soon seated and looking out over the harbor at the boats and enjoying her hot bowl of gumbo.

And this is all part of the job, she thought to herself. *I get to eat whatever I want, and it is company paid.*

Jackie felt incredibly lucky indeed and grateful for an opportunity like this. She was happy she decided to take the leap and try out for this company. She never imagined how fantastic it would turn out to be. Jackie ordered a beer when she was done with her gumbo, enjoying the view until the sun completely set.

She paid her tab and began her trek back to the hotel, feeling light and happy. Jackie was unaware of the man lurking ahead in the shadows until she was on top of him and he pulled a knife on her and demanded her purse.

Sobering quickly and realizing she let her guard down, she laughed out loud, confusing the would-be robber. Jackie told him to go away, but instead, he lunged at her. She quickly disarmed him and put his own knife to his neck. His eyes opened wide in disbelief as he heard Jackie say, "Now will you go away?"

She took his knife and continued down Pratt Street as though nothing had happened. Still stunned, the robber-turned-victim sat on the sidewalk and watched her go.

CHAPTER 29

Upon returning to her room, Jackie giggled to herself. She was a bit giddy knowing she was not scared and could react quickly and effectively. Her confidence was riding high, as she finally felt completely safe for the first time in her life.

She turned on the bathwater and decided to soak in a bath despite having already showered. She would enjoy her downtime. She would watch a movie afterward if something good was showing. She picked up the movie guide to see what was playing just as her phone began to ring. It was Helga.

"Hello," Jackie answered.

Helga congratulated her on the successful completion of her assignment and said to expect a knock at her door with another envelope for her next task. Before Jackie could respond, Helga hung up the phone and the knock struck as though it were Helga herself at the door.

Jackie approached the door and looked out the peephole, fully expecting it to be Helga, but it was an older woman with a manila envelope in her hand. She opened the door and retrieved the envelope, and without a word, the woman retreated down the hall toward the elevator.

It all seemed dramatic to Jackie, but nonetheless, she still liked all the mystique. Sitting cross-legged on the bed, Jackie unsealed the envelope containing her new assignment.

> Car—Silver Porsche, NY handicap tags in parking spot B721, door PIN 9876, keys under the driver's seat.

Hotel—Hilton Times Square, NYC. Your room key will be on the phone app. Clothing—All needed for this assignment will be in your NYC hotel room.

Subject—Ricky Wasser, successful, popular rock star from Manchester, England.

Details—Ricky Wasser recently released a recording that was hugely controversial. Listen to the song "It Was Bound to Happen" for reference.

Jackie stopped and pulled up Spotify on her phone and plugged in the song to listen. She read along with the lyrics as the song played:

So many lives
So many chances
So many ways
This could've been prevented

Western world dominate
We don't think we discriminate
But we do
We always do

It was bound to happen
New York's towers crumpled
The London Bridge laid red
Paris's concerts bled

We all trembled and said
The blame lay with them
They said the blame lay with them

We interfered they believe
With how they conceive
Their country be run
The West brought the gun

And now we forget
We should all work this fret
Come together and see
We all should seek peace
It was bound to happen.

Wow. This was not an easy song to listen to. Her ire was up over this song too. She read on to see what her mission was to be.

> Ricky Wasser will be playing a concert in Madison Square Garden. One show on Saturday night at 9:00 p.m. There is expected to be massive demonstrations and a lot of news coverage. He does have a lot of fans here in the United States who get his purported message of working toward peace, but many more find him to be a closet radical.

> Your job will be to get him into the venue undetected and out undetected. Wasser will have an adjoining room at the Hilton. You will get him from the room to your car at 7:00 p.m. and drive him to the venue, where you will park as though you are a patron and walk together into Madison Square Garden. Another security detail will take over at this point.

> You will then be in the mosh pit next to the stage throughout the show. The show should end approximately 10:45 p.m. At which time, he will reach down in the pit and pull you up on stage.

You will act like a super fan and be excited. You both will exit the back of the stage and change into a new set of clothes so that you may leave in the same way you entered.

Allow at least half an hour before your departure so as not to be stuck in the parking garage. If you find you are jammed in, do not return to the car until you can exit quickly. You will then drive him back to the hotel and the following morning to JFK International Airport where his private plane will be waiting. Follow the signs to the cargo area, and then you will be directed to the correct terminal for Mr. Wasser's plane by the ground crew. You are authorized to use any force necessary to protect Mr. Wasser.

Interesting, she thought.

She had never met anyone famous before. Jackie turned off the water for the now-filled tub and disrobed for her bath. She brought the file to read again while she soaked and decided she would leave in the morning for New York City and get a good sense of the path between the hotel and Madison Square Garden.

For this detail, she would need to know the way to Madison Square Garden and alternate routes as well without use of a map or GPS. Quick reaction and fast driving would be the method of protection for this asset. Jackie laid the file down and eased down to her neck in the tub and closed her eyes, enjoying the soothing of hot water on her tired body.

CHAPTER 30

Jackie woke with a start. She thought she had overslept, but her alarm had not yet sounded for 5:00 a.m. She rose anyway and sent for a pot of coffee and some rolls, glad she had twenty-four-hour room service available.

The coffee arrived quickly, and she drank a cup before donning her workout clothes and heading to the hotel gym. She used the treadmill first, clocking in five miles easily as she listened to music in her ears. Next would be the weights. There were few weights to work with, but she improvised and managed a decent workout.

Back at the room, she took a quick shower and put her hair in a ponytail and started the packing process. Even though the clothes would be left behind, she would need the toiletries and makeup. She also grabbed an extra bottle of water for the car.

She turned on the early news while she sipped a second cup of coffee and ate a Danish. The news was reporting that a woman had been shot and killed at a concert inside Hampton Coliseum last night. The woman tried shooting up the stage during an Ellee Morena concert and was stopped by her security. The news team flashed to a picture of a sobbing Ellee Morena and standing at her side, to Jackie's delight, was a stoic-faced Allison.

"Go, girl!" Jackie said out loud, happy to see Allison's success.

Having finished her breakfast, she switched off the TV and grabbed her small bag and headed to the garage. There in spot B721 sat a beautiful Porsche, and Jackie again could not believe her luck. What an incredible car! She could not wait to hit Route 83 and 95 to see how it handled.

Jackie accessed the car through the remote entry pad and pulled out of the garage slowly, excited yet nervous she could bump the car into a concrete column. She headed over to Lombard Street and then turned left on President Street to get onto Route 83N.

Jackie was anxious to test the curves with this beast of a car. She was not disappointed, thoroughly enjoying the curves that wound out of Baltimore, until the flashing lights appeared in her rearview mirror. Laughing, she pulled over, knowing it was her own fault.

Jackie took her time driving to 695 and then 95 north toward New York. Once she got past the White Marsh area, she floored the gas pedal once again. There was extraordinarily little traffic on the northbound side of 95 and she hit 100 mph in no time. She enjoyed the fast speed for a few more miles before she slowed it back down.

Another speeding ticket cannot be good for the job, she thought.

A few hours later, Jackie was inching through the Lincoln Tunnel into Midtown Manhattan. Following her GPS, she easily located her hotel and parked in the first handicapped spot in the garage. She located her seventh-floor room without any issues.

Inside the room, Jackie found the clothes she would need for this assignment: jeans, a see-through lacy shirt with a black bra to be worn underneath—*Sexy*, she thought—Dr. Martens boots, and a crossbody handbag.

Looking at the handbag, she saw it had a quick gun release and tested it. *Nice*, she thought and loaded her personal items in with the gun in preparation for later. There was also a cane with her clothing, which must be why she had handicap tags on the Porsche. There was a note detailing the cane's composition of steel to be used as a secondary weapon should it become necessary.

Jackie looked out her window onto Times Square and was dazzled by the brilliant display of neon billboards. Being her first time in New York City, it was such a spectacle to behold. She decided to go down and experience the hustle and bustle of the streets outside her window and search for something to eat.

Her food selection was made easy by the fact that there was a pizza restaurant about every other block. How could she resist? Having filled her belly with the greasy goodness, she headed back to her room to learn the route for tomorrow evening inside and out.

Jackie plugged in Madison Square Garden in her GPS, and off she went the nine blocks, barely half a mile. She wondered if it would be easier to walk the short distance, but that was not her decision. She timed the lights down Seventh Avenue to Thirty-First Street then back up Ninth Avenue. This was easy with the grid layout of the streets. The only issue would be traffic. Jackie returned to her room to study the map, making sure she knew the city enough to get them away safely should the need arise.

CHAPTER 31

Saturday seemed so far away when Jackie first received her assignment. But it was here now, and she was on to Ricky Wasser and what appeared to be an easy assignment. She had just gotten back from a run on the hotel gym's treadmill when she heard the soft tapping at the adjoining door. Annoyed that her time was disturbed before the commencement of her services, she talked through the door.

"Yes?" she asked.

"It's me, Ricky Wasser" she heard in reply. "Can you open the door a moment?"

Jackie opened the door and recognized the man on the other side from the photos as Ricky Wasser. He was short and skinny. Maybe cocaine-skinny; he was so thin. His hair was dyed jet-black in contrast to his very pale skin. He wore jeans with holes in them, not unlike the ones chosen for Jackie to wear to the concert. He topped off the look with a plain black T-shirt.

Jackie introduced herself and held out her hand to the gaunt man.

He shook and replied, "Call me Ricky. I just wanted to see you before we headed to the show. You never know what the security company sends over, and I want to be sure you can indeed defend me."

"Don't judge a book by her cover," replied Jackie, already disliking him.

He was condescending for a scrawny man needing her for protection. Jackie knew already she was not going to enjoy his company.

Ricky smiled and replied, "Touché. Would you like a drink with me? A little icebreaker?"

"No, thanks," replied Jackie. "I'm just back from the gym and need to get things together, but I will be ready promptly at 7:00 p.m. to escort you as contracted. Enjoy your afternoon."

And she closed the door and slid the lock in place then rolled her eyes.

Jackie turned on the TV so that she would not be eavesdropped on as she went about getting a shower and dressing. She wanted to eat dinner before work and decided to order up from room service. Another encounter with Ricky ahead of time was something she wanted to avoid.

She sat on her bed watching the news as she ate a light dinner of salmon and vegetables. The evening was going to turn chilly she saw as she pulled on the jeans. She searched for a jacket and found one hanging in the closet that would work with the outfit.

She slid a knife into an ankle holster and fastened the holster in place. With the gun already in her bag, she stood to leave.

Ready for work, she thought and smiled.

Jackie grabbed the walking cane and knocked on the adjoining room door promptly as promised.

Ricky was wearing a ball cap and dark sunglasses as well as a large sweatshirt. It did the trick at concealing his identity, as he did not appear to be that frail little man she had met earlier. Jackie took his arm and guided him toward the elevator. They exited into the garage and hopped in the Porsche without passing anyone.

Slowly, Jackie drove the route to Madison Square Garden as she had planned. They entered the building hand in hand without as much as a single glance from the protestors or media crews who lined the sidewalk. Once inside, Ricky was handed off to his stage security team, and for now, Jackie's job was done.

Jackie squeezed into the mosh pit with a rowdy group of young people singing along and dancing to the opening band, Handshake, as they concluded their last song. She managed to work her way to the stage front just in time for Ricky's entrance in a flash of pyrotechnics and smoke. She propped the cane weapon in front of her and against the stage wall.

Jackie screamed like a rabid fan, jumping up and down to the beat of the music, feeling the others bump into her as they did the same.

If nothing else, I am getting a great workout, she thought.

When the show had ended and after his last encore, Ricky grabbed her hand and hoisted her up out of the pit and onto the stage. She quickly grabbed the cane as she rose and limped to Ricky's side. Feigning excitement to be chosen, she watched as Ricky signed off, then they retreated to the rear of the stage.

Once backstage, Ricky donned the old sweatshirt, hat, and glasses. Jackie added a sweatshirt and cap to her ensemble to ensure anonymity. Ricky threw instructions around to the pack up crew as they waited patiently for the crowd to leave. Forty-five minutes later, Jackie and Ricky strolled hand in hand to the garage and the parked car, again without notice.

Jackie eased the Porsche out of the garage and headed up Eighth Avenue toward Times Square and the hotel. They easily made it back to their rooms undetected. Jackie was pleased with her job and would complete it in the morning with the drive to the airport.

She closed and locked her room's adjoining door. Ricky had already locked his side. She sat in the quiet room for a few moments, enjoying the lack of noise, except for the residual ringing of her ears. That was when she heard Ricky talking to someone in an excited tone on the phone.

Jackie moved closer and pressed her ear up to the wall to listen. Her gut was telling her something was off about this conversation, and she wanted to discover what that was exactly. His voice had a very urgent tone, and what she heard next stunned her.

"Fucking Americans. They have no clue. Their heads are buried in the sand. They will not see this one coming or suspect it was me who orchestrated it. Just carry this out as I've instructed."

That was enough to alarm Jackie, and she moved away from the wall.

She switched on her TV and called Helga to report back that she had safely returned the asset and what she had just overheard. She was stunned at the turn of events, believing Ricky to be an idiot who got lucky with music. To her surprise, Helga responded that Ricky Wasser was, in fact, on the government's radar as a terrorist threat.

"We suspected his US tour was a front," she said.

Jackie's head became overwhelmed with questions, and she flooded Helga with those now. "Government radar? Am I working for the US government? Why was this not shared up front?"

Jackie was suddenly feeling very confused and borderline angry.

Helga responded, "Now is not the time to have a meltdown, Jackie. There is a vital task at hand, and yes, we are both working for the US government. I will answer all your questions when you get back to Baltimore, but for now, I need you to follow my instructions quickly and carefully. We need to stop Ricky Wasser from this imminent attack. Agreed?"

Jackie replied, "Agreed."

"We believe we know who Wasser is working with and have other assets on those suspects too. But right now, we need you to interrogate him for information that could be pivotal in stopping the threat we believe will take place within days."

Helga took a deep breath and continued, "I need you to gain entry to his room by whatever means necessary; find out the information on who, what, where, when, and how; and then put a permanent stop to this traitor. Then carefully lock up and check out of your room and head south to our office. Can you do this? This is a matter of national security, and you are perfectly positioned to act.

"Jackie, you do realize you have had extensive and detailed training for just such an event, and I firmly believe you can handle what I am asking of you. I am sorry to spring this on you, but you must see I had no choice with this matter being presented as it were. We, at the agency, had hoped to offer you this position once you gained more experience. But again, we did not expect this situation to arise, and we must act."

Jackie was reeling.

Is this actually happening right now? Can I interrogate and then assassinate someone?

She could hear Wasser's laughter over her TV program. Was he laughing at the US? Deep down, Jackie knew she needed to at least explore this and interrogate Wasser. And she knew she would complete the assignment if she found that Helga was indeed correct and he was a terrorist with an imminent plan of attack against the US.

She gave her assent then hung up the phone. Jackie pulled the knife from her ankle and cut off the power cords to the lamps in her room and slipped them all in her back pockets. She then stowed her hotel key in a front pocket and took a deep breath to help ease her trembling hands and rapped on the door. Ricky quickly opened.

"Sounds like you were having some fun over here, and I thought now that we are done working that maybe I could join," Jackie said and smiled.

Ricky smiled and swung the door wide for her to enter, clearly thinking it was his lucky day.

"I have some amazing tequila if you're interested," said Ricky.

"Absolutely!" said Jackie.

As Ricky turned to pour Jackie a shot, she pulled a lamp cord from her back pocket and quickly wrapped it around his throat, holding tight until he passed out. She loosened her cord and eased him to the floor then used it and the other cords to tie him up.

When he came to a few minutes later, her first words were "Of course, we have a fucking clue."

Ricky had a panicked look come across his face.

Perfect, Jackie thought. *He is scared.* "You know why I'm here, right, Ricky?" she asked as she traced around his left eye with her knife.

Ricky muttered, "I'm not sure."

Jackie pierced his skin with the tip of her knife just under his eye. Tears started flowing over the cut, mixing with his blood and making a pink stream down his cheek.

Jackie said, "I need all the details of the attack you so arrogantly claimed we have no clue about of course. At the risk of sounding cliché, we can do it the hard way or the easy way. But we are going to do this quickly, as I am well aware that time is of the essence."

Ricky responded without hesitation, "Fuck you!"

"Yes! I was hoping I could have some fun before you forked over the information. Be right back. Now don't you go anywhere, sweetheart," she said with a wink and a smile.

Jackie went to the bathroom, wet a washcloth, and returned.

"Are you sure you want to do this the hard way?" she asked, and as Ricky opened his mouth to answer, she stuffed the wet rag into his mouth.

She then turned up the TV to help mute the noise that was about to take place.

She stood over him and said again, "Are you sure?"

And before he could answer again, she grabbed a fistful of hair and pushed her knife into his face, just below his eye but still in the eye socket. She carved from left to right as though she was applying eyeliner. Ricky's screams were very muted.

"Hang in there another minute, Ricky. I need more supplies. Be right back, okay?" she said sarcastically.

Jackie took the ice bucket from the table to the tub and filled it with water and grabbed a hand towel. She returned to see the pink stream had turned very red now, flowing down his cheek to his shirt where it had begun to absorb and fan out like spider veins.

"Ready?" she asked brightly when she returned.

He shook his head vigorously, but Jackie ignored him and continued. She soaked the water out of the ice bucket with the hand towel, placed it over his face and forced him backward to lie on the floor. He was screaming through the washcloth in his mouth, but Jackie just said, "Ricky, I really can't understand you when you have something in your mouth. Did your mama not teach you any manners? First, cursing. Now this?"

She stretched the towel to cover his terrified eyes and began to pour the water slowly. After a few minutes of this, she removed the washcloth and pushed him to a seated position and removed the other washcloth in his mouth.

Ricky choked and pleaded with her to stop.

Jackie replied, "But you said you wanted to do this the hard way, Ricky. Have you changed your mind now?"

Ricky nodded furiously.

Jackie said, "I'm just not sure you are ready. You say you are, but I am going to need some convincing that you are going to cooperate fully."

Once again, Ricky opened his mouth to speak, and once again, the washcloth was stuffed in. Ricky screamed as Jackie pushed him on his back a second time, covered his face, and began to slowly pour the water. Returning him to a seated position again, Jackie said, "Well, spill it already, darling, unless of course you are enjoying this."

Ricky listed the names of the accomplices he was working with along with the dates and manner of the attacks planned into Jackie's phone so she could record the information. One attack was for New York City the very next day. They intended to set off a bomb on the red line as it approached a subway stop in Midtown Manhattan.

Having gotten as much information as she thought he had, Jackie said, "Thank you for your cooperation with ensuring the safety of United States citizens. And on behalf of them, I would like to extend my gratitude for your involvement in this matter," and with that, she slit his throat.

Jackie emptied and dried the ice bucket and put the two wash-cloths in the bathtub. Careful to not leave fingerprints, she then ransacked the room and took his cash. Lastly, she swapped the lamps from Ricky's room for the cordless ones in hers, before locking the connecting door.

Having completed her assignment, Jackie quickly packed up and left, checking out on her phone app as she drove toward the Lincoln Tunnel. On her way back to Baltimore, Jackie called Helga from the car to report the task had been completed and played the recording of her interrogation. She hung up and sank back into her seat, feeling exhausted with all that this day had thrown at her. She played no music. She drove the speed limit; she was numb for now.

CHAPTER 32

Jackie wholeheartedly believed she needed to do what she did, but her life had just changed. It had changed without her consent and without her foreknowledge. She felt blindsided. Not in a million years did she see this coming. She was very unsure how she felt about the job going forward. On one hand, she felt empowered. On the other, she felt like she had no choice in this.

Jackie swung the Porsche into the first handicap spot at the company's Patterson Avenue offices. She walked in the door and scanned her security card and said hello to Mark, who guarded the offices. Normally, she would flirt a little, but today had been too overwhelming.

Mark noted the change and wondered about its cause. Jackie rounded the corner and headed toward Helga's office. It was early, almost 4:45 a.m., but Helga was there waiting. Helga knew she had to do some damage control, but of course, it was all part of their plan.

"Sit down, Jackie. I know this has been an exhausting day, an unexpected day for you. Being up all night doesn't help one to think clearly either."

Jackie took the offered chair and asked, "Why wouldn't you have said this was a government-run business? Why the secrecy in that?"

Helga replied, "Let me tell you a story. There once was a man whom we all knew to be a terrorist. He trained killers in Afghanistan and Pakistan. Our laws do not allow for assassination just because we know he is building a network. No, my dear, they do not. This man was on everybody's radar, but we simply had to wait to see if he acted or if he deployed men to do harm to our country or our allies. And acted he did on a grand-scale. You know of whom I speak, I am sure. Countless times, we could have eliminated this threat, but we followed our laws and allowed the attacks to happen. Only then could we justify our actions, which of course eventually happened with SEAL Team 6. Because of this, President Graham put together a program under the guise of this security agency to help us protect our country and our allies from future attacks when we know them to be imminent. Yes, we do also have assets to do security jobs, as was the case with John Hansen for you. But our main purpose is to protect our country and allies both in the US and abroad. You should know that you had in-depth training geared toward this work and excelled in it. In fact, you are one of the best to ever work our program, and we are extremely excited to bring you on to our team if you so desire. We hope you desire it."

Jackie took a deep breath and exhaled.

"So does this mean I would be a spy? An assassin? What would be the job requirements?"

Helga smiled inside, knowing she had effectively brought Jackie into the fold.

"You would be all that but masquerade as a security asset. You will receive your assignments in the same manner as before, only they will be targets, not customers. You will be given intelligence briefings and locations of the target. Only there is never a story to go with the assignments as it was previously. You will not be given reasons or explanations for the execution of any task. Merely what you need to complete it. Can you do this job and be a part of keeping our country safe?"

Jackie felt a wave of patriotic pride sweep over her as she nodded her acceptance. She was still confused and hoped she was making the right decision. But protecting her country could not be wrong if this was a government operation. Her wandering mind came back into focus as Helga tapped on her desk.

"I knew we could count on you, Jackie. Welcome to the real team," said Helga. "Now I imagine you are exhausted. Please take the next couple days to relax and rejuvenate. Your phone should have your room ready for access at the downtown Hilton. You will be contacted there for your next assignment."

Jackie thanked Helga and retreated to the Porsche. She drove mindlessly to the hotel and crawled into bed and slept through the afternoon until evening.

*****

Jackie pulled on a pair of jeans and took the mile-long walk over to the brokerage. She found that PBR and Howl at the Moon were both closed this evening to her disappointment. It was Sunday she remembered and backtracked to the Cheesecake Factory for dinner.

While eating her food and watching the busy harbor, she thought that a boat might be nice. A big one for the times when she was home and in between assignments. She would love to fit some river or bay cruising into her summers, as it far outweighed the option of living out of a hotel room. She decided to investigate this and see what it would take to make it happen.

CHAPTER 33

Mark Adams was puzzled. He had always had a friendly work relationship with Jackie during the brief time she had been on board and was surprised at the lack of cordiality from her. Today, she seemed agitated and distracted as she headed for Helga's office, so he listened closely to the ensuing conversation.

Mark had been the duty guard at Henderson and Associates for a few years now. He was assigned this job amid hushed whispers of a rogue program, which, of course, turned out to be completely true. Mark usually knew some of the details of the operations handed out to assets, as he had bugged both the director's and Helga's offices as instructed. He walked around with an earpiece that listened all day, unbeknownst to anyone but the admiral who had sent him there.

His reports of the program in the beginning of his tenure were quite disturbing. He was fully astonished that the higher-ups decided to let it continue. The only explanation given to Mark was that the girls had already endured the abuse. "Let us see if we could find the silver lining and get some really good assets out of this program," they said. But continuing the program would not be part of the plan, and at some point, it would be completely shut down.

Always one to obey orders, Mark continued his daily surveillance and daily reports.; He believed the admiral would know what was best. It was not his job to question authority; just follow it.

Today's surveillance was a doozy. Mark had pressed the record function to capture whatever was going on because of Jackie's entrance and knew all hell could break loose in there. He listened as Helga managed to manipulate Jackie to bring her on to the assassin's side of Henderson.

Impressive job, he thought.

Mark did secretly admire Helga for her audacity and effective management skills. She made people quake in their shoes, and rarely had he heard someone say no to her. And when he did hear the occasional no, that asset was never to be seen again.

Mark believed he admired those qualities in Helga because he did not possess them himself though he wished he did. He had been powerless to leave the program and this double life. Mark once tried, but the unidentified admiral demanded he stay. Of course he acquiesced, which brought him to this point today.

As he listened to the conversation further, Mark found that Jackie, too, could not say no to Helga. Helga always got her way. Mark often wondered if Helga would ever say no to the director or contradict him in any way. The only person who could bring Helga down a notch was the director.

The director demanded everyone's full attention, and no one would dare to divide it. All who encountered him agreed that he was a scary man. But if Helga stood up to him? Well, that would definitely be a confrontation to end all confrontations. He laughed to himself. He would love to record that conversation if it ever happened.

Mark also had another secret. During his second month of work in the Baltimore office, he was approached by an ex-employee of Henderson and Associates named Carter Grayson. Carter was forced to retire because of his adamant refusal to go along with the Franklin Project, but he did not just go away like the rest of the employees did who were forced out.

Carter watched the comings and goings from a distance, gathering information and following assets as much as he could without being detected. But he could never get any definitive information that would expose the Franklin Project that he knew existed. So he approached Mark with the request that he divert some of the information he overheard to Carter.

Mark was easily persuaded, as he was not happy with the program still in play despite the admiral's assurances that it would end in the near future. With promises from Carter that Mark's name would never be revealed, he began his triple agent life—the one who guards at the headquarters, the one who reports back to the admiral on all assignments, and the one who feeds information to Carter in hopes that the Franklin Project would be revealed and terminated.

CHAPTER 34

Three days later, Jackie woke to an early morning knock at her door. She peeped out to see the same woman who delivered assignments as before. Jackie opened the door, and the woman handed over an envelope and a small suitcase. She took both and retreated into her room. She dropped the suitcase on the bed and eagerly slit open the envelope.

This was a more precise directive:

> Target—Carmelo Escararo Location—Guayaquil, Ecuador
>
> Your identification—Felicia Sanchez. You are required to dye your hair deep brown. Use the enclosed self-tanner to darken your skin and the contacts to change your eyes to brown. See passport photo for guidance.

Intrigued, Jackie read on.

> Target will be traveling in a black Range Rover, license tag 68490392 over the Puente Guayaquil Samborondon Bridge on Friday at approximately 4:00–5:00 p.m., local time. The bridge is always slow due to the volume of vehicles. Your target will be most vulnerable when he approaches the east end of the bridge.

Your flight leaves from JFK tonight at 9:12 p.m. Boarding pass and passport enclosed.

Return flight leaves Guayaquil Friday at 7:22 p.m. Boarding pass enclosed.

When you arrive at the José Joaquín de Olmedo International Airport, exit the southeastern side and get a cab to number 78 Palmer del Rio. The house key will be under the sixth pathway square. Inside will be all your supplies needed for this job, and any updated information should it come to light. Leave all Jackie Ford identifications in your room as well as your weapons. Everything needed to travel to the location is included in the suitcase.

Be safe.

Be smart.

Jackie opened the suitcase and dumped the contents on the bed for inspection. She found four sets of brown contact lenses, mahogany-brown hair dye, and the self-tanner as well as clothes, sandals, sunglasses, and sun hat.

She opened the passport and looked at her picture. She hardly recognized herself with the changes to her coloring.

The agency did an excellent photoshop job, she thought.

Jackie set all the documents on her bed and reached for the phone to order a fresh pot of coffee and some eggs. She needed to get the cobwebs out of her sleepy brain and wrap her head around her first assignment of this type. She knew she had the grit to do this job but struggled with accepting the new role as her way of life.

In retrospect, Jackie fully realized that Helga had manipulated her into this position, but that was most likely the only way she would have ever considered such a profession. Had Helga come out at the beginning and said, "Jackie, how about you be an assassin for the US government?" she felt positive the answer would have been no.

Jackie pushed aside the internal turmoil and ate her breakfast. She picked up the assignment and read it again. She was certain she could fulfill this directive if she could learn how to turn off her conscience and not think too deeply about the assignment. Jackie closed her eyes with this new realization, and within her soul, she flipped the switch.

Wasting no time now, Jackie began the process of dyeing her hair the mahogany-brown color that was required to match her passport. Once done and her hair up in a towel, Jackie applied the self-tanning lotion and watched her skin darken. She applied more tanner until she achieved the tone that she thought most closely matched the image in her passport.

Next she blew her hair dry and was amazed at the difference a color change could make. She liked the contrast of her blue eyes with this hair color. She popped in the brown contacts and, to her satisfaction, saw her new identification completed.

Jackie Ford was now transformed into Felicia Sanchez. She enjoyed the transformation and hoped all her assignments would involve a new identity. It was like getting into a Halloween costume. She busied herself with memorizing the details of her new persona for the next couple of hours then decided to test herself on the knowledge during her flight to Ecuador.

CHAPTER 35

Transformed and eager to experience a new country, Jackie, now temporarily Felicia, opened the trunk of the Porsche and placed her suitcase inside. She set her GPS and headed out of town for JFK airport. Once on Route 95 north, Jackie again sped up to enjoy the car's ability. She adored this car and kept it up at 110 mph for the next 10 miles before slowing it back down.

Hopefully, I will always be assigned this vehicle for my tasks, she thought.

Pulling into the long-term parking lot, Jackie was right on schedule. She got her suitcase from the trunk then walked to the nearest airport transit stop and sat on the bench. The sign above was counting down to the next arrival, and it showed three minutes.

Three minutes would be enough time to check her phone for messages. None. She felt lonely for a second then let the feeling pass. There was a lot to look forward to in her life currently. Friendships could wait until she was firmly entrenched in the job. Her job was important; it mattered.

Jackie decided to look up boats. She knew absolutely nothing about boats, but she wanted to learn. Having a boat on the water seemed amazing. She typed in "boats for sale" in her browser and up popped a plethora of options. She closed the phone to save it for her downtime. It was simply too much to decipher right now.

The bus arrived as promised. Jackie hauled her suitcase up the steps and found a seat next to a young couple, clearly going on their honeymoon. They grinned at each other and held hands the entire ride to the entrance. Jackie could not help but smile herself as she caught herself staring at them.

The airport was mobbed, more crowded than she had ever seen at her hometown airport. Jackie searched out and found the shortest line to get cleared through security. An hour later and through that security, she plopped in a seat at the first bar she saw and ordered a Guinness. She would have to kill a couple of hours before boarding would begin.

Jackie looked up to request a menu and thought she saw Allison sitting opposite across the bar. They stared at each other. It was definitely Allison. Jackie hesitated a minute, unsure of the protocol for contact, before she decided to stride over and sit next to her.

Smiling and feeling genuinely happy to see her friend again, Jackie quietly began, "I saw the Hampton Roads Coliseum report on the news. Well done." She looked at Allison and saw distance in her eyes, unaccepting of the praise. "Are you okay?" Jackie continued.

Allison looked directly in Jackie's eyes and said, "It's been a hard adjustment knowing I took a life."

Jackie was surprised, as that was not her feeling being in the same position.

"It was your job to protect, and you did that. That is the gold standard right there, Allison. You have done very well. You should feel empowered, proud, stronger. Yes, it is never a good feeling to take a life, but you must remember you saved a life too. One that you are paid very well to protect."

Allison paused to consider Jackie's perspective, and a thoughtful expression was evident on her face.

These are the words I needed to get over this hurdle, she thought, glad Jackie had found her sulking in this bar.

She knew she needed clarity to continue this job.

Allison changed the subject and asked, "Where are you headed? Next assignment?"

"Sure am, South America. How about you?" asked Jackie.

"I am off to protect the children of actor parents in LA. Hopefully, this will be an easy one this time around," replied Allison.

Jackie realized that Allison had yet to be brought into the covert government side of the business. Perhaps that was not in the cards for Allison and she would stay on clients for the overt side.

"I like your hair color change. It looks like you've had an assignment in an island somewhere," Allison replied in a whisper.

"It's self-tanner," Jackie laughed. "I dyed my hair dark, then felt I looked way too pale, so bought some skin color."

Allison laughed for the first time, and they eased back into conversation like their training days.

Time flew, and Jackie's flight was now called for boarding.

She hugged Allison tight and whispered, "Stay strong. You are amazing at your job."

Then she exited the bar and headed to her departure gate.

CHAPTER 36

Allison had looked at her assignment before entering the bar in JFK airport where she ran into Jackie. It appeared to be nicer than her previous one of guarding a rap star.

> Location: 2334 Central Greens Way, Los Angeles, CA
>
> Subject: The Coleman Family
>
> Joe and Linda Coleman may be known to you as actors. They are currently working on a joint venture to act in and produce a movie. They are away from home for extended periods and wanted extra protection for their children.
>
> You will fly to Los Angeles and be picked up by their car service. At the Coleman home, you will be given a bedroom and bathroom to use during the terms of the agreement. It will be your priority to protect this family, and deadly force is granted should the need arise.
>
> Be smart.
>
> Be safe.

Clearly this would be a posh job in Allison's eyes. She was looking forward to getting to know the family and living in a warm, sunny area.

Allison left the bar and headed toward her terminal at the opposite end of the airport. She had just settled into one of the cramped seats when she heard the boarding call for first class. Grateful she had this luxury, she stood and got in the short line.

CHAPTER 37

As Jackie settled into her first-class seat, she again thought she was fortunate to find this job. She was living the high life when not working. The flight was easy but had some turbulence, as it began its descent into Guayaquil, and the plane touched down roughly. The line was short at customs, and she was through without incident. Glad to be on solid ground now, she began to follow the plan details previously laid out for her.

Jackie exited the airport as instructed and jumped in the back of a cab waiting at the curb.

"Seventy-eight Palmer del Rio," she uttered as the driver pulled into traffic toward the airport exit.

The cab was old and had no air-conditioning, and it did not take long for Jackie to perspire.

As they crossed the bridge of her assignment, Jackie took note of their speed. Everyone drove about ten to twenty miles per hour because of volume. This was good for her plan. When they approached the end of the bridge, there was also construction to add to this confusion and speed reduction.

The cab dropped Jackie off, and she waited for him to speed away before she lifted the sixth paver to find the key as described. She entered the sparsely furnished and thankfully air-conditioned home. She investigated the first floor where she found a small sofa and TV in the entry living room and a pub-style table with two chairs in the kitchen.

She opened the refrigerator and saw that it had been stocked with little food and drink, just enough food and drink to see her through the assignment. She was to be at this location for a day and a half to complete her assignment.

Next Jackie climbed the stairs to the upper level where there were two bedrooms. One was completely empty, the other had a small bed. There was one bathroom where she found one towel and washcloth sitting on the sink. In the bathtub, there was just a single bar of soap.

In the corner of the empty bedroom, she saw steep steps and climbed those to see where they went. They led to a partially finished attic where she found a sniper's rifle, telescope, and an envelope. She peered through the telescope and saw it provided an excellent view of the bridge.

This was to be Jackie's first assassination, not counting the accidental assignment of Wasser. She was a little excited to use the sniper rifle and happy it would be a hands-off kill. She was giddy to feel the power of life and death once again in her hands.

She opened the envelope and read the contents:

> Target has changed cars to a blue Audi X7 with license tag 07446582. See photo. All other details remain the same.

Jackie liked the detail change, as the car was less common here than the first. She did not recall seeing any Audi SUVs on her way over, but of course, she was not looking for them.

She returned to the telescope to ensure she could discern tag numbers and verified that she could. She picked up the sniper rifle and looked through the scope, again pleased. Now it was to be a waiting game.

Jackie backtracked down the stairs to the bedroom and realized there would be no clean change of clothes.

Oh well, she thought and turned on the shower to heat up the water.

She would shower anyway and let her clothes to air out a while.

Feeling refreshed and in her underwear, Jackie returned to the kitchen to eat. She made a sandwich of turkey and Swiss cheese, switched on the TV, and curled up on the sofa. To her amazement, there were English subtitles on every station, and she wondered if

Helga had ordered them. Or did the last asset who used the house set the controls closed-captioned for English? Either way, Jackie was grateful.

She settled for a movie called *Holiday*, a coming-of-age story set in Ecuador. Jackie must have fallen asleep, she realized, as she woke to gunfire that seemed too close for comfort. She turned off the TV and crept over to a window to peek out onto the street where she saw two men jumping into a car and driving off. There was a third man shot, lying in the street, blood quickly pooling around his body. Sadly she knew she could not help the man, as it would jeopardize her cover.

She made sure the entire house was dark and sat up until sunrise, nervous she could be caught in the cross fire of a retaliation. The commotion out front started shortly thereafter, and she dared a peek outside to see police and the coroner cleaning up the area.

Suddenly, someone rapped loudly at her door startling her. The police, she deduced. Jackie remained quiet and still until they walked to the next home and began the process of rapping loudly again. Thankfully they were done with their investigation and cleanup and were out of the area by noon. Her plan would not be delayed.

*****

Hungry again, Jackie ate an apple and another sandwich. She knew she would not be able to eat again until her return flight to the US, so she piled the remaining turkey and Swiss onto her roll. She switched on the TV and mindlessly watched a daytime drama while she ate her dagwood sandwich to kill time. And time was not kind. It seemed to drag on and on today.

Finally, it was 3:00 p.m. and Jackie got into position in the attic to begin her watch. Several Audis had crossed during the watch before her telescope clearly found the target as it began to cross the bridge at 4:05 p.m. She confirmed the tag number and tried to locate the target himself.

Jackie jumped on the sniper rifle as the car neared the middle of the bridge and picked up her target again. Slowly the car advanced, and slowly Jackie followed along through the scope as it made its way with the traffic. As the car approached the construction zone, Jackie acted and squeezed the trigger.

A second later, she watched the target slump over in the front passenger seat with blood pouring from his temple. The chauffer panicked and hit the gas to escape but collided with a fuel tanker that was stopped in front of him. The ensuing explosion blew the construction barriers upward with the car as though escorting the pieces of the vehicle into the air.

Having prepared for her exit, she left the house and traveled by foot southeast to find the second bridge that crossed the Daule River, south of the one currently burning. She saw a cab as she approached Biblos Street and hailed it. The cab deposited her at the airport a couple of hours before her flight was scheduled to depart. So far, everything was going according to the plan perfectly.

Jackie made her way through security and sat in a lounge by the gate and watched the news coverage of the unexplained explosion that just occurred, also reporting that Carmelo Escaroro, a prominent businessman, and his driver were both presumed dead. She could not make out much more than that with the language barrier. But she did note that people murmured all around her in disbelief.

She called Helga and reported that the assignment was complete, and she was currently awaiting her return flight at the airport. Jackie sat quietly while she waited, nervous she would be discovered as the killer she was. It felt like people were looking too closely at her, but she realized that she was being paranoid.

CHAPTER 38

Helga hung up the phone and smiled. Jackie had indeed proved to be the prodigy they envisioned she would become. This was a test to see if she could handle an assassination without getting her too close to her target. They needed to know if Jackie remembered her training and could perform as a sniper. It would be necessary for future assignments the director had in mind.

Helga walked down the hall to Jack Franklin's office and knocked for entry. Jack called for her to enter, and she folded herself neatly in the chair as she always did.

"I saw the report on the news," began Jack. "So she has passed her first test?"

"Brilliantly," replied Helga. "Jackie is proving out the program as a success."

"Have you assessed Allison yet?" asked Jack. "She has turned the corner and regained her confidence by all appearances. Of course, we will not know definitively until we put her to a more stringent test."

"Shall I begin that process now?" asked Helga.

"Yes. Have someone grab one of the kids she is guarding and see how she reacts. If she is unwilling to use deadly force, we will keep her on the protection team for the time being," replied Jack.

He brushed his hand in dismissal, as was his way to end meetings.

Helga put the test in place as ordered. The poor, unsuspecting employee who drew the job was told it was a hostage-negotiation practice and not to concede to the demands to let the child go. And so, the next day, he would be completely fearless in the execution of his assignment.

CHAPTER 39

Allison had settled in like family with the Colemans. She learned to be apart yet not apart and always in the background, watching. She learned to be discrete when it came to Linda and Joe and retreated to another room whenever they shared affection.

Currently, the two were working on a film together locally in Los Angeles, and Allison was enjoying hearing the daily insider's information on the progress. Dinners were always noisy with the kids chatting away about their days and Linda and Joe laughing about the most current debacle on set.

One sunny afternoon, Jessica, the nanny, took the children to a nearby park, and Allison stood close by in the shade of a palm tree to watch. She was feeling a lot happier being around this family during the last couple of weeks. Allison wished she could have had this kind of family when she was growing up. There was so much love.

The children were easy to love too, and she found she had a favorite in the youngest—four-year-old Lily. Lily was very carefree and always up for a trip to the playground. Her wild hair and big eyes were the same cinnamon color of her skin. Allison nicknamed her the chameleon, partly because of her coloring and partly because of her great ability to hide in plain sight when the children played hide-and-seek.

But Lily's favorite thing was the monkey bars at the park, and that was where she was currently. Lily bobbed from bar to bar with a seriously determined look on her face that made Allison smile.

That child will have a huge drive to succeed in the future, thought Allison.

Suddenly, a man ran quickly up to the monkey bars and snatched Lily off. He ran toward a white cargo van parked about a hundred yards away, and Allison tore after them. Lily began to scream and cry in fear as Allison yelled, "Stop, or I will shoot you dead!"

The would-be kidnapper turned to face Allison and placed a knife to young Lily's neck.

Lily cried, "Alli, please come get me. The man is scaring me."

"I will get you, Lily. Just hang on one minute while this man sets you down," Allison replied.

The man laughed. "Not happening, I will cut her throat first."

Tears were streaming down Lily's face, causing Allison to focus. She aimed her firearm at the man's forehead, terrified she would hurt the girl she had come to love. Allison spoke to the abductor.

"I will give you to the count of ten to set her down," she said in the sternest voice she could muster. "One, two—"

The man laughed.

Allison continued, "Three, four."

And she then squeezed the trigger.

Both the man and Lily fell to the ground.

Allison quickly scooped her up so that Lily would not see the carnage next to her. Lily hugged her tightly as they headed toward the car where Jessica had already corralled the siblings.

Jessica had summoned the police immediately, and Allison dialed Helga to report the incident. The police quickly arrived, and Allison provided a description of the events as well as her identification and the details of her assignment to protect the children. The police took statements from the other park patrons who all corroborated Allison and Jessica's account of what happened. They were asked to be available for follow-up questions should they arise then permitted to leave.

The family departed and went straight home in a dead silence, most surely in shock. Linda and Joe arrived shortly after the kids. There was a collective sigh and cry as they came together and hugged.

Joe mouthed, "Thank you" to Allison, who brushed away a tear and mouthed back, "You're welcome."

Allison felt the buzzing in her pocket and pulled out her phone. It was a message from Helga. She requested Allison to return to the agency once her replacement arrived.

*****

The next day saw the arrival of Allison's replacement. She was another agency woman named Laura Stone. Laura was tall, being close to six feet. She had long light-brown hair, beautiful big brown eyes, and an easy smile that Allison was happy to see. The kids had been traumatized and needed some softness until they healed.

Laura handed Allison an envelope with her flight boarding pass for her trip back to Baltimore. Allison filled Laura in on what had transpired and then gave her a rundown of the family's needs. She showed Laura to the room where she stayed and began the packing of her belongings, randomly throwing things in the bag. She took down the pictures the children had made for her that were posted on the wall and tucked them in too. She left with promises from Laura that she would take excellent care of the family.

CHAPTER 40

Allison felt a huge rush of relief as she hopped into an Uber for her ride back to LAX Airport. Her flight was in about two and a half hours, and she should have just enough time to make it. After checking in her weapons, she was escorted to the gate for boarding, making it with little time to spare before the doors were to close.

She eased into her first-class seat and welcomed the drink offered by the flight attendant. A moment later, she called the attendant back and requested some vodka, which she promptly dumped in her soda. She needed to unwind.

The events from yesterday were surreal.

It really happened, she thought, and then she brought back to mind Jackie's comment on how it was her job to protect. This time, she really felt as though she had done the right thing.

Just imagining Lily alone with that pervert was enough to make her nauseous. Thank God she did not flinch and her shot was true. She was going to miss this family and of course Lily, but she also understood that she would be a constant reminder and that would not be helpful for the family to heal.

Allison settled into her seat and pulled her phone to check messages. There was one from Helga:

> There will be a red BMW M3 in long-term parking lot B right next to stop 7.

> MD tag number CP7 000. Lock code 7000. Keys will be under driver's seat.

Take the car to the Hilton in Baltimore, and use
your phone app to access your room.

Take an extra day to unwind and report to the
office at 9:00 a.m., Wednesday.

Allison was happy to see she would have some time to get herself together before having to report into the agency.

The plane touched down at 8:40 p.m., and Allison was feeling
exhausted. She retrieved her weapons and suitcase and stood for the
bus to long-term B parking. She was looking forward to sleeping and
adjusting to the time change.

The car was easy to find at stop 7, exactly where Helga had
said. She got behind the wheel and pulled onto Route 170 and drove
quickly to the hotel.

Allison was pleased to see snacks when she entered her room,
having not eaten on her flight to the East Coast. She had some cheese
and crackers and a few sips of wine before she fell asleep with the TV
on, fully dressed.

CHAPTER 41

The sun was blinding Allison, and she realized she had neglected to close the shades in her room before she fell asleep. She did so now and headed for the bathroom. Her clothes were damp from sweating heavily while she slept, so she decided to strip and get in the shower.

Breathing deeply and pulling the steam into her lungs was cleansing. The water felt like a gift from heaven as it washed away the grime and renewed her spirit. Her day was going to be a lot better. She was sure of that.

Later that morning, Allison nervously exited the hotel, worried that some of her boxing buddies might see her. The gym was too close for comfort. She hoped the baseball cap would be enough, and she tucked her hair up into it before she left.

She headed down Pratt Street toward the inner harbor. She needed the fresh air, and it had been ages since she walked around the pavilions there. Allison entered the Light Street Pavilion and walked the distance down the center aisle. She exited onto the brick pavement and decided to head toward the Science Center.

*****

The day was bright and sunny, and the water looked cleaner than she recalled. The surroundings were refreshing and soul pleasing, so she walked on. She continued past the Science Center and toward the Rusty Scupper Restaurant. Feeling a new energy engulfing her now, she decided to turn up Key Highway and continue her walk, clearing her head of the anxiety from California.

It occurred to her that she was at a turning point in her career. She was well on her way to being an experienced, seasoned asset. This thought served to buoy her confidence as she strode purposefully up toward Federal Hill.

Suddenly, in her face was a knife held by the dirty hand of a white man about her height. He had snuck up behind her while she was lost in thought. His face was deeply lined, and his greasy long hair was pulled back into a ponytail. He quietly urged her to hand over her purse and she would not be hurt.

Without thinking, Allison grabbed the knife quickly from his hand and held it to his neck and said, "How about you give me your wallet?"

The man looked terrified then turned and fled. Allison was determined to not let her day off be ruined by this.

Along her way to Federal Hill, she found a restaurant called Little Havana. She went inside to order some lunch. She had never had Cuban food before and went with the popular Cuban sandwich. It was not a mistake, as the sandwich was amazing.

The return walk to the hotel seemed to take a lot less time. Allison resisted the urge to head west and visit James and the gang though it pulled mightily on her heart strings. She entered a hotel room that seemed quiet in comparison to her walk and switched on the TV for the noise. She soon found herself absorbed in the movie *Message in a Bottle*. Kevin Costner was making her cry harder than she should have been.

She realized she was reacting to the previous event in the park, but part of her also knew she was lonely for companionship. She missed James. That was all there was too it. Feeling melancholy now, Allison decided to order room service and stay in for the night.

CHAPTER 42

Allison pulled the red BMW into a parking spot at the agency, arriving fifteen minutes early for her 9:00 a.m. appointment with Helga. She scanned through security and headed toward Helga's office but was greeted in the hall.

"Follow me," said Helga.

Together, they walked farther down the hall and knocked on a door that had a nameplate that read Jack Franklin, Director. Allison heard a deep voice beckon them both to enter. They took seats opposite Mr. Franklin, and Helga spoke first.

"Mr. Franklin, this is Allison Kincaid."

Allison extended her hand to shake. Jack took it, not missing the firm confidence it revealed.

"Good morning, Ms. Kincaid," he said. "I hope you are settling into your role with our company nicely."

Allison replied, "Yes, sir, I am. Thank you."

"I requested to meet you after your heroic measure to protect the young girl in your charge. We as a company are proudest when our youngest of clients are protected. You represented us extremely well, and I wanted to personally congratulate you on a job well done."

Allison felt pride surge inside herself as she thanked the director for the accolades.

"I was doing the job I was trained to do, sir," she further replied.

"Your training, yes. I was looking over this." Jack held up a file with her name on it. "It shows you excelled in your training especially in marksmanship."

"Thank you, sir," she replied.

"I am wondering, Allison. Are you a patriot?" he asked.

Allison was quite taken by surprise at the question, and the confused look must have been evident on her face as he continued.

"Do you believe in the US government?" he asked.

"Of course, I do, sir," she responded.

"How about our military? Do you agree that our military is the best in the world and, as such, it is our obligation to help the US and our allies with protection against their enemies?"

"I must admit I hadn't given it a lot of thought, but generally, I would agree with that," said Allison.

"Good answer!" exclaimed Jack.

Jack was carefully grooming Allison, aware that she was not ready to be an assassin, but she would be soon.

"We sometimes help out with situations of national security, and I needed to be sure we were in agreement should the need arise to use you in this capacity."

Again, Allison was taken aback but replied, "Of course, sir. However I may be of service."

Franklin waved his dismissive hand, and Helga stood to leave. Allison jumped to her feet, too, and they exited the director's office.

Back in Helga's office, they sat opposite each other at her desk.

Helga began. "It is very unusual for the director to request to speak to an asset. You should feel honored."

"Yes, I do," responded Allison, smiling.

Helga pulled an envelope from a tray behind her desk and slid it over to Allison.

"Your new assignment. Take it back to the hotel and read it. You are dismissed."

"Thank you," replied Allison.

She rose and left the office and the building. She drove back to the hotel and walked quickly to her room, eager to read the new assignment.

Now seated on her bed, she ripped open the envelope.

Location: Winchester, Virginia

Hotel: Hilton Garden Inn, 120 Wingate Drive

Subject: Ben Saunders, owner of Saunders Farms

You will use the BMW car to drive to your hotel. There you will find a blue 1983 Chevrolet pickup truck with Virginia license plate number ZRW 928. The door will be unlocked and the keys will be under the floor mat. You are to use this truck until the completion of this assignment.

Ben Saunders has solicited our help because of a death threat he received from one of his migrant workers, Romero Sanchez. Sanchez was released from service when he was caught stealing apples. Sanchez's picture is enclosed, and there is no criminal record.

Ben Saunders believes the threat to be credible and has received numerous phone calls threatening his life.

You will be prepared to work as an apple picker on this farm alongside Saunders as well as local and migrant pickers. Other farm duties may be requested at Saunders's discretion.

You are authorized to use deadly force if necessary.

Be smart.

Be safe.

Allison set the directive on the bed next to her.

A farmer? she thought. This assignment did not seem like it would be fun.

She realized there was a suitcase sitting next to the desk, and on top of the desk was a long wooden box. Curious to see what else Helga had in store for her, she opened the box and found a rifle and scope.

Delighted, Allison pulled them from the case to examine closer. Rifles were her favorite weapon in training, and she hoped there would be an opportunity to at least shoot this one.

She saw there was also a small, subcompact 9 mm handgun and a knife with sheath for her belt that she did not initially notice. Those would be perfect to have on her body while she worked the farm.

Next she opened the suitcase. Within, she found a few pairs of denim jeans, a few plaid flannel shirts, a few T-shirts, and a worn-looking Kenny Chesney ball cap. There was also work shoes and sneakers to complete the persona.

Initially Allison was not thrilled about this assignment, but then she reconsidered. When would she ever have an opportunity to experience working on an apple farm again in her life?

She changed into a pair of jeans, flannel shirt, and sneakers then packed the rest of her belongings back into her suitcase. She balanced the long box on top of her suitcase and rolled the two down the hall to the elevators.

Once loaded in the car and on her way, she tuned into 93.1 on the radio to listen to country music.

"Yee haw!" she muttered out load.

CHAPTER 43

Saunders' Apple Hill Farm was not the pretty homestead that Allison had envisioned on her drive west. It was not abysmal, but it was not beautiful. Some of the perimeter fencing sections looked rotted or broken. The barns desperately needed a fresh coat of paint, and there was mud everywhere.

Allison parked the old blue truck in the gravel driveway and walked up the steps of a huge white farmhouse. She knocked on the black-painted door.

At least the house looks nice, she thought as she waited for a response.

From within, she heard a woman's voice yell, "Coming!" and the door swung open.

Mrs. Saunders was a beautiful middle-aged woman of about forty-five years. Her brown hair looked disheveled even though it was pulled back into a ponytail. She was tall and thin and had brown eyes that smiled continuously as she spoke her greeting.

"Hello. You must be Allison Kincaid from the agency," Mrs. Saunders stated.

"Yes, ma'am, I am," replied Allison.

"Well, come on in and get acquainted. Ben is out picking with the workers. He is great like that. He believes he should have a hand in picking apples during the harvest season and puts in a hard day's work like everyone else. My name is Judy by the way. Are you thirsty or hungry?"

Judy was very welcoming to Allison, and she was soon caught up in idle conversation over a piece of apple pie and a cup of coffee. Again, Allison felt herself being drawn into a client and getting emotionally invested. She wondered if she needed to check herself somehow, but she did not. There was no way of knowing how long this assignment was to last, so she may as well enjoy the time.

An hour later, Ben Saunders came through the door. His bulky frame took up the doorway, and his sweaty clothes put off the smell of the day's hard work.

"Pie!" he exclaimed and pulled his cap off his head and sat next to Judy at the table.

Judy's affection for Ben was visibly evident as she planted a kiss on his cheek and served pie to her husband. Ben, too, had smiling eyes, and Allison thought, *This is what a happy couple looks like.* Judy introduced Allison and gave some background information while Ben ate.

Once done the pie, Ben got straight to business.

"First of all, you need to know how to pick apples. I will take you out and show you shortly because not only will you kill our next year's crop if done incorrectly, but you may give yourself away as not being a picker. We work from sunrise, which is about 7 a.m. currently, until 11 a.m. for lunch. Lunch is half an hour. Then back to work until 5 p.m."

Allison listened quietly to Ben's instructions.

"Our days are filled with conversation and sometimes music. But we work hard together and value each other's contributions. So it was hard when I saw Romero walk to a row of previously picked apples. I knew he was not as invested in the group as the rest of us, but I did not think I would find he was filling his own basket with apples. I cannot tolerate mistrust in my crew, and I fired him immediately. And now you know the rest of the story."

"I will have a rifle in the rack of my pickup as well as a handgun and knife on my person. I am very well trained to protect you should Romero return to cause a problem," Allison assured Ben and Judy.

They nodded their heads in understanding.

"Now let us go learn how to properly pick apples," Ben concluded.

CHAPTER 44

Allison pulled into the farmyard at 6:45 a.m. She figured being a little early would give her time to further assess her surroundings. There were a group of workers walking toward the trees where they left off from the previous day's harvest. Ben came from the nearest barn to greet her, carrying a ladder.

"This is for you," he said. "We are on the fourth lot of trees where you see all the ladders. Choose the next tree and start picking."

Allison chose her tree and started up the ladder when she heard a friendly voice.

"Hello. I am Sella from the tree next to you. Where are you from?"

Allison provided details learned long ago in training, and the women chatted and worked through to lunch.

Every year, Sella came back to this farm to pick apples. She said the owners treated the workers very well, and she enjoyed working outside. She lived in the area and was married with four children, all under the age of ten. Her husband, Eduardo, was working on the next tree line over.

The lunch provided—baked chicken thighs, spinach, carrots, and corn bread—was surprisingly delicious. Someone had set up a radio that played classic rock music, which provided a nice background for the meal.

Allison and Sella returned to work side by side after lunch. When their day had ended, the women exchanged their goodbyes. Allison offered the couple a ride home, but they declined, saying they worked out the kinks by walking.

Back at the hotel, Allison stripped her grimy clothes and eased into a hot bath. Her arms were not used to the motion of picking apples, and they were exhausted. She thought about her day on the farm and decided it was not so bad after all. In fact, she rather enjoyed the work and comradery.

Day two turned into a month, and it looked as though the end of picking was near. Allison by this time had assumed the threats of Romero Sanchez were just that: threats. Nobody had seen or heard from him in weeks, and she believed her employment would also stop with the end of picking season.

Allison's assumptions were wrong. During a lunch of turkey and ham sandwiches, she realized that Ben had not joined them as he usually did. She told Sella that she needed to talk to Judy about something and was going up to the house.

As she approached, she saw Ben being propelled to a barn about a hundred yards away and realized she had let her guard down. She quickly skirted the back side of the house then raced to the barn that Romero and Ben had just entered.

Knowing there was no time to wait, she walked in and called out for Ben.

"Ben, we ran out of water at lunch. Where can I find more?"

Romero answered in a loud voice, "Ben is occupied at the moment. You need to leave the barn."

"But we need the water," she replied then advanced toward them.

Romero brandished a knife and again told Allison to leave.

"Why would I leave if it is obvious you intend to harm Ben?"

The response bewildered Romero, who was not used to a woman challenging him. He thrust the knife at Ben's stomach and again told Allison to leave. Allison simply said no.

Romero pushed the knife into Ben's stomach and Allison rushed him. She knocked Romero to the floor and fell awkwardly next to him. They both rose quickly to their feet and faced each other. Romero was enraged as he charged Allison who sidestepped and tripped him back to the ground. In the process, her handgun, which was tucked in her waist, flew across the dirt floor, out of reach.

Ben had moved to a chair next to the barn wall where he pulled the knife from his belly. The knife was small and had not penetrated deeply, but it bled profusely anyway. He watched as Allison continued her struggle to get control of Romero.

Allison watched as Romero rose once again and laughed at her misfortune of losing the gun. She warned Romero to settle down so that nobody else got hurt. His response was to throw a kick at Allison's leg. She had not anticipated the kick and buckled to the ground. Romero pounced and pushed her backward on her back, but Allison continued his motion into a roll and ended up on top.

It was then she realized that Romero had stabbed her in her side. He had a second knife. Quickly she unsheathed her knife and returned the favor, stabbing Romero.

She asked, "Have you had enough?"

Romero responded, "No," and threw a jab at Allison's jaw.

She felt her head snap back as Romero pushed her off. Romero suddenly slumped over to the right. Allison had landed a cut to his femoral artery, and blood was spurting as Romero watched in horror. He tried to stop the flow, but it was just too much, and he fainted.

Allison stood and called 911 to request the police and an ambulance. She looked at Ben, who was pale with shock, and assured him he would be okay. Her side did not hurt until this moment, but it was throbbing now. She then called Helga to report what had just transpired.

Once they were through with the police and the hospital, Allison returned to her hotel to pack up. She showered and readied everything for an early morning departure. She needed the rest, and Helga had requested she come straight to the office for a debriefing.

CHAPTER 45

Allison felt awkward behind the wheel of the BMW. She had become used to driving the clunky old pickup truck for the past month. It did feel good to be in a smoother ride though, and she cruised easily eastward back to the office, arriving about 7:00 a.m.

Inside she was greeted by Helga, who displayed her pleased look for Allison. Again, she was beckoned to go right away to the director's office.

This is getting to be a habit. I wonder if he does this with everyone, she thought.

"There is a reason I asked to speak with you besides to congratulate you on a job well done in Winchester. You have shown you are ready to advance to the next challenge in your career. I would like to promote you into our covert government program as a terrorist asset. Would you be interested?"

"Absolutely, sir," responded Allison, surprised and nervous to accept the advancement offered to her. *Wow*, she thought, *I will now be involved in secret security assignments to fight terrorism.*

"Helga will supply you with all the details of your new position. I knew you were going to be special when I saw your scores from training, and I expect great things from you. Thank you for your patriotism," said Jack as he closed her file.

Allison glanced downward with his motion and noticed Caron Tucker/Jackie Ford on a second file and the words *successful induction* written at the bottom of a notepaper clipped to the front. That added to her excitement, as it appeared that Jackie might also be working with her on the anti-terrorism unit.

Allison stood and shook hands again before leaving the office. Inside Helga's office, Allison took a seat to hear more details of this new position, unable to keep still from excitement.

Helga again welcomed Allison to the unit and further explained that her alternate identification learned in training was the beginning of this process. She would have other identities that she must be able assume quickly. Every job could have a different identity and background story.

Of course, there would be a significant pay raise and she would also be keeping the BMW as her own car. The job would include international assignments from time to time, and she immediately realized that Jackie was doing exactly that when she last saw her.

"You will be given assignments in the same manner as before. You will complete them without question, as the details are usually not known to us. If at any time you do not believe you can perform the task requested, you are to contact me immediately. Is that understood?"

Allison agreed, and Helga offered an envelope and a suitcase.

"I happen to have your next assignment ready, so I will not be sending it by courier. Take this back to the hotel. The key is on your phone as usual. Do you have any questions?"

Done with the promotion details, Allison rose and thanked Helga. Mark waved to her as she exited, already knowing what just took place from his eavesdropping. This young lady seemed sweet, and he hoped she could handle what was about to be thrown at her.

CHAPTER 46

Mark gathered up what was once again incomplete evidence for Carter. He always heard conversations about the aftermath of assignments and heard persuasive arguments designed to bring assets over to the assassin side of the business, as he did today, but no hard, indisputable facts that specifically referenced the Franklin Project.

The only real assignments he heard were legitimate security needs. And Mark could never get hold of one of the envelopes he saw assets leaving with to read its contents. Carter took the information nonetheless and started a letter-writing campaign, citing the information he did have in hopes of scaring Franklin into at least halting the program.

What Carter truly lacked was the evidence of how Franklin facilitated the program. Who were the assets who followed out the heinous orders that allowed the project to proceed into his twisted vision?

He needed recordings or written documents of how Franklin intended to find the parents of the newborn, drug-addicted girls in the local hospitals and pay them off, essentially having access for training the girls from birth.

Carter recalled the details laid out by Franklin and how horrified he was at the level of violence he intended to inflict on these children. It was unconscionable. It was madness. Anyone who had objections were dismissed by way of forced retirement.

The violent nature of this proposed project was what stuck with him and drove him to bring the devil down. Carter was 100 percent sure that Jack Franklin was indeed the devil. He bowed his head and prayed, not for the first time. Carter begged God to help him in his endeavor to put an end to the Franklin Project.

CHAPTER 47

Feeling a fresh sense of purpose, Allison dropped both the envelope and the suitcase in the trunk and returned to her hotel. Excitement was an understatement for her. She could not wait to read her assignment and raced up to her room.

Dropping the suitcase inside the door she ripped open the envelope.

Target—Juan Tesquer

Allison dropped the paper, alarmed. *Am I a government assassin now?* The thought had occurred to her as Helga laid out the responsibilities. She reached to retrieve the paper and read on.

Location—Bogota, Colombia

Your identification—Emilia Socrates

You are required to wear brown contact lenses and wear your hair curly. See UK passport photo for guidance.

Target will be in Lillaluz Park most evenings after 5:00 p.m. where he skateboards.

Your flight leaves from JFK today at 5:20 p.m. Boarding pass and passport are enclosed.

Return flight to be determined upon completion of task.

You will arrive at the El Dorado International Airport and take the shuttle to the Hilton Garden Inn, Bogota. There will be a Do Not Disturb placard on your door. Leave it there for the entirety of your stay for this assignment. Use your phone app to unlock the door. You will find further details in your room.

Leave all personal items except what is in your suitcase here in Baltimore, including your Allison Kincaid identification.

Be safe.

Be smart.

The realization sank in fast that she was indeed a government-sanctioned assassin.

Am I now the "ghost" I have heard people speak of before?

She remembered a story James had talked about and how you never know who the ghosts are. It was all a secret and how they rid the world of its most vile people without detection.

Will I be able to do it?

She considered the events of the past few days and knew she had no problem using deadly force. But unprovoked could be hard. She knew she did not have much time to make up her mind, but she sat on her bed anyway, not even opening the suitcase. She needed to let this sink in.

Half an hour later, Allison opened the suitcase, knowing she had accepted her new role. It was filled with clothes and shoes and a couple of hats. The contacts were in the front zipper compartment, and she pulled them out to try a pair on. They darkened her eyes to brown. There was a curling iron as well as old-fashioned pink foam roller curlers to make her hair match her passport. She plugged in the curling iron to begin her transformation to this new role.

*****

Allison was seated next to the window on her flight and looked out at the mountains of Columbia as the plane descended.

Such a beautiful country, she thought.

On another occasion, she thought she might like to visit and hike those hills.

Her plane landed a little ahead of schedule, and she disembarked to locate her suitcase. The shuttle was already at the curb when she exited the airport, and she hopped on, not uttering a word during the short ride there.

She entered the lobby and was happy to see there was a small bar to the right. It might be nice to have a few drinks later tonight to calm the nerves. She found the elevators and went up to her room on the eighth floor and entered with her app key, leaving the Do Not Disturb sign in place as instructed.

On the desk, there was a long box, much like the one that held the rifle in Winchester. She opened it and found a few weapons—a knife with a sheath to conceal inside her pants' waistband, a small pistol with an attachment to silence its noise, and a long-range sniper rifle.

There was also an envelope, and inside it read:

> Target tends to skateboard most evenings from 5:00–6:30 p.m. in Villaluz Park, which is walking distance east of the hotel. You will need to scope out the best options to effectively carry out your task using any weapon from the box.
>
> It is pivotal that you carry this out without being detected. Once completed, return the weapons to the box, lock it, and contact Helga for further instructions on your return flight. You have five days to complete this assignment, but the sooner the better.

Allison checked her watch. It was 4:00 p.m., so she decided to find the park immediately. She wanted this assignment to be behind her as quickly as possible to prevent her nerves from messing her up. She pulled her curly hair up into a ponytail and donned sunglasses, dressed in running clothes, and left the hotel.

Looking at the local map she grabbed in the hotel lobby, Allison knew she needed to cross the bridge over Calle 26 and continued onto Transversal 85 until she reached Calle 63F, where she would turn right and head into the northwest corner of the park. She memorized the directions then began her journey.

The park itself was only about eighteen square blocks, so she was sure she would not have too much trouble locating her target. She began to jog, enjoying the environment until she needed to jump into surveillance mode.

She managed a couple of miles before she saw the caravan approach and knew her target had to be within. Sure enough, there he was. He exited his vehicle right behind his security detail. Skateboard in hand, he walked over the grass to the pavement and dropped it down, toeing it a little before hopping on top.

Allison followed along, running fast at times so as not to lose sight of her target. She noted her options and thought a knife was out of the question. A sniper shot would be hard to accomplish as there were no high points or buildings where she would not be detected. So the pistol will have to be the weapon of choice, she concluded.

As she rounded another corner, she also noted that most corners had four feet concrete columns as street markers. She decided she would use one to obscure her shot then continue as though she was just jogging. To her advantage, the park echoed with loud noises, making it harder for the security detail to pinpoint any noises that might occur.

Plan in place, Allison returned to the hotel. After her shower, Allison headed to the bar. Riding the elevator down, she thought better of the decision and returned to her room where she ordered room service. The less exposure to people, the better, she figured. Plus, tomorrow would be an anxious day. She should keep her head as clear as possible.

She settled in for the long night and made a mental note to bring a book next time to help fill the void. She wet her hair and rolled it up into the pink cushion rollers. For this trip, she would watch a lot of movies on her phone, as she did not understand the language of the country. Maybe play a game or two. She used to love tri peaks solitaire.

She settled on the solitaire and got lost in that game for several hours. Once tired of games, she switched to movies. Finally sleep overcame her, and she fell asleep with the Disney movie *Mulan* playing in her earbuds.

CHAPTER 48

Today is the day, thought Allison as she came fully awake.

She pulled the curtains opened and enjoyed the mountains off in the distance. She would eat a hearty breakfast and nothing else until her target was terminated.

Contrary to yesterday's long day, today flew by quickly. Allison put on her running clothes, carefully choosing a dark-colored, loose-fitting shirt to conceal her pistol. She tucked the weapon into her compression shorts and let her tightly curled hair stay loose. She put her iPhone earbuds in both ears and headed out for a "run."

It was close to 5:00 p.m. when Allison entered the park and began as she had before. She saw the caravan approaching her, and she mouthed words as though she was singing along to a song. There was no song in her ears. The caravan stopped, and as before, the bodyguards exited first then the target.

Tesquer dropped the skateboard and took off quicker than the last time. Allison could not keep up. She tried her best not to panic, knowing she had a few more days to complete the task if today did not work out. She would need to be further into the park for the next opportunity.

She continued to run to keep up her cover as a park runner, and to her surprise, the target flipped around and stopped. Today, it would appear, was a day to do tricks. Tesquer was spinning and jumping the board over benches. He looked almost angry as he completed his tricks, not pleased with his own abilities.

He skateboarded toward the column Allison was about to pass, and she knew her moment was here. She slipped the gun from her shorts, stopped briefly to take aim, and hit the target once in the head and once in the chest.

Allison quickly threw the gun into a bush, turned up the music, and continued her run, picking up her pace to distance herself from the gun. She was singing out loud to a chorus of a Muse song when she felt her shoulder grabbed and she was spun around.

She snatched the earbuds out and could still hear the music blasting away. The bodyguards began patting her down simultaneously, and she feigned fear and pleaded for them to leave her be. The guards were unconvinced she was innocent and escorted her to their SUV.

Real terror began to set in, but then she reverted to her training. She remembered why it was so important to know her cover identification so well as she pleaded for her release. The guards loaded the dead body of Juan Tesquer in the back like a sack of potatoes, not taking care, as Allison would have thought they would.

Next they indicated she should get inside, but she shook her head and became hysterical. She saw that there was another man sitting on the car's bench seat with his hands tied together and looking equally scared. A victim of being in the wrong place at the wrong time, she knew. She had passed this man while she was running. She suddenly realized and became worried he might have seen something.

Allison looked at him with pleading eyes. He just looked down at his lap. Allison was picked up and shoved into the SUV, then the doors were slammed shut. She was trapped and totally under their control now.

The prisoners rode on in terrified silence. The driver would occasionally look in his rearview mirror at them, and Allison made sure the tears were flowing. She hoped that she would be able to save the man that was caught up in her mess, but she had serious doubts.

About twenty minutes later, they pulled into the driveway of an enormous estate with a big cast-iron *T* on the gate. They were met in the driveway by two additional men, and the security guards jumped out to share the news of the boss's death.

It quickly became evident to Allison that this had to be a drug cartel.

Did I just kill a kingpin? she wondered.

He was too young to be the head of anything. Perhaps a son?

The house guards came over and looked inside the car at the two prisoners and ordered they be brought inside. They were marched into a room off the foyer with a blue tiled floor and scant furnishings. The windows were wide open, allowing a breeze to raise goose bumps on Allison's wet skin.

One of the house guards dragged a chair to the center of the room where there was a small settee. Looking both his prisoners over, he chose Allison to sit first.

Allison started crying anew and said, "I'm just a visitor out for a run in the park. Why are you doing this to me?"

He forced her to sit in the chair and wait as two men entered the room. One was tall with pale skin and awkward looking in a loose-fitting suit. The other looked to be a servant in a blue uniform.

"What is your name?" requested the taller of the two men in a heavily accented voice for Allison.

"Emilia Socrates," she replied.

Her hands had not been tied, and she pulled her little concealed passport holder out and showed them.

The servant stepped forward to retrieve it and looked it over before he passed it around to the others in the room. The tall man took a seat on the settee and laid the passport beside him. He then began with questioning Allison.

"Why do you kill this man? Who do you work for?" he demanded.

Allison sprang tears from her eyes once again.

"I didn't kill anyone. I was just running in the park. I didn't even know anything had happened because I was listening to my loud music. Then the men snatched me and made me come here."

The man stood over Allison and pulled his hand back and landed a slap on the side of her head that sent her to the floor, screaming in pain. She looked up and pleaded once again that she did not do anything. The man indicated she return to her chair. Allison complied.

"Once again, I will ask you, and you had better tell me, or this will only be worse for you. Who do you work for?"

Allison replied. "Please, sir, I am on vacation. I am a writer for the *London Times*. Nothing more."

The interrogator turned to another of the guards and said, "Take her to the red room. I will send Ivan to extract the details."

With that said, Allison went crazy, sobbing and begging, and was dragged from the room as the interrogator indicated to the other prisoner to take a seat.

CHAPTER 49

The red room turned out to be a shed in the rear of the house. Allison assumed the name was given because of the amount of dried blood she saw on the floor as the guard opened the door. She could only imagine the atrocities that took place here and wanted no part of it.

She turned to face the captor and pleaded once more.

He looked at her with blank eyes and said, "The hysterics won't work on me. Get in there."

She then asked if they both were going to hurt her, knowing he would turn to see who she meant by "both," as he was the only one escorting her.

He did turn, and Allison acted decisively. First, she chopped his throat hard with the side of her hand then landed a fully loaded kick to his groin. He dropped to the ground, attempting to moan and breathe at the same time.

She slid his knife out of his belt and finished him off with a quick slice to his carotid artery. Allison got the gun that was tucked in his pocket and crept toward the road. She was unsure of going out into the woods behind the house, not knowing where that led and chose this path instead. She would have to be on full alert because she was sure it would not take long for them to see what had happened. She was glad to be in a running attire, knowing now that she was running for her life.

Once to the road, Allison headed in the direction they came. She had paid close attention during the drive, knowing she may very well have to get herself out of this predicament. She ran as fast as she could but was still in earshot and heard the alarm sound for her escape.

Knowing she could do her fastest running on the road, Allison stayed there until she heard the motors start. She estimated she was only a mile into her estimated ten-mile run back to the hotel.

As the cars headed in her direction, Allison headed into the woods and away from the road. She climbed a tree and stayed still until the cars had passed. They would know she could have only gotten so far, but she was fast and sprinted through the bramble like it did not exist.

The cars returned to check the other direction, and once again, Allison hid in a leafy tree. She continued advancing like this until she got to the perimeter of the park. By then, she hoped the security team had assumed that she was hiking through the woods and believed she would never make it.

They did, however, patrol regularly between the park and the house, searching until it was dark. In complete darkness, Allison located the discarded gun and risked exposing herself by running across the bridge to her hotel. She had been hiding and observing and too fearful to leave her safe spot. But the darkness covered her enough to make it back to the hotel.

She slid out the phone she had also tucked in her shorts and entered the room. She immediately called Helga.

"Target eliminated but with complications," said Allison.

She went on to give Helga a rundown of what had transpired and requested a new passport.

*****

Two hours later, there was a knock at her door, and there on the other side was Allison's new identity to get her home. She took the envelope and suitcase and closed the door. Inside the envelope, she found a passport for Theresa McCormick, US citizen. Her hair was a strawberry-blond color, so Allison figured she knew what was in the suitcase.

She opened the suitcase, verifying the hair dye was in fact inside along with new clothes. Allison hopped in the shower to shampoo away her curls and wash the sweat from her dehydrated body. She dyed her hair as quickly as she could then blew it dry. She removed the brown contacts and let her eyes return to their natural green color.

The time on her flight boarding pass was too close for comfort. She needed to catch the airport shuttle immediately. She quickly dressed in a dress designed to add about thirty pounds to her frame and exited the room. The Do Not Disturb sign fluttered on the door handle as the it slammed shut.

Walking through the lobby with suitcase in hand, Allison noticed one of the men from Tesquer's house posted near the door. Her heart raced as he considered her then continued his scan of the area. She felt fortunate to have made it into the hotel earlier before they posted the guard to look for her.

Allison confidently walked past the sentry and out onto the sidewalk to the waiting shuttle for the airport. Her disguise worked perfectly.

CHAPTER 50

I am on an adrenaline high, thought Allison as energy surged through her body.

She was unable to stay still in her seat, which, for the first time, was not first class. Probably because of the last-minute purchase, she surmised.

She was sandwiched between two small women and conceded in her mind it could be a lot worse. She put her earbuds in and listened to music to avoid the inevitable conversation that always happened when you are so closely seated. An hour later, her plane mates were talking over her as she fell asleep.

Back in Baltimore, Allison picked up her car and returned to her room at the hotel. She settled in and expected a phone call, but none came. Surely after this accomplishment, Helga would want to speak to her. She was too wound up from Bogota, so after waiting a couple of hours for the call that never came, she went for a walk.

Walking down Pratt Street for the third time since she started working at Henderson, she saw James coming toward her. It was too late, as he clearly saw her first, and his face was lit up with a huge smile. At first, Allison panicked but then allowed herself to run into his embrace. She had missed James dearly, and tears sprang from her eyes.

"What's all this fuss about now, girl?" asked James, giving Shelly the once-over. "When did you get back in town? Where do you live now?" he asked.

Shelly responded, "Just in town now. I am here for the company headquarters. I have a meeting in the morning."

James peppered her with questions, and before she could answer any, Shelly just laughed.

"I'm guessing you can't tell me a lot of this, can you?" James finally asked.

"No, I really can't. But I can tell you I am doing very well. I feel like I am contributing something important to society now. You always told me that would be an important thing for me to learn to do."

James smiled wide again. Allison knew he was happy his teachings had sunk in. They did not always with his strays, he had told her.

"Do you have time for supper?" asked James.

"I wish I could say yes, but I am not supposed to have contact with my old life until they grant me that privilege."

James's smile turned to a frown. He did not like the sound of that, but he did not press her either.

"But you know, James, that you will be at the top of my list when that happens."

His smile returned, and he hugged her again.

"Keep safe, little bird. And keep in touch whenever you can," James said and continued up Pratt Street.

Allison felt renewed by the encounter and hoped to see James again soon. Turning onto Light Street, Allison decided to slip into Sullivan's Steakhouse for dinner. Her appetite was huge, and a nice rare steak was just what she wanted.

CHAPTER 51

Director Jack Franklin was furious, to put it gently. His face bloomed a beet red as he pushed the intercom button and beckoned for Helga to come into his office. Mark listened as he heard the details of what he gave to Carter be read off from a letter received that morning along with the warning to stop the program immediately before the letter writer turned over all information he had in his possession.

"Who is the leak?" demanded Jack.

Helga stared in disbelief, her face igniting too.

It can be any one of the assets considering the information exposed, she thought.

But first, she was more concerned with the author of the letter and said as much.

"We should start with the group of employees who retired. Do you recall anyone as being more agitated about retirement than the rest?" she asked.

"No, they were all idiots," Jack responded.

"I will pull the files of the retirees and look through the notes and try to determine which order to start the investigation. I will also pull in every asset who had an assignment mentioned in the letter and do a lie detector test," said Helga, and she left to begin the work.

CHAPTER 52

Jackie had only been back a day from Ecuador when she received her next assignment in London. She was feeling the jet lag from the back-to-back trips and looked forward to a long sleep.

As her plane touched down at BWI Airport, she heard a ping on her phone for a message. She saw it was from Helga. It read: "Drive directly to the office from the airport for a debriefing."

Great. Just what I needed right now, she thought.

Jackie exited the plane and decided to eat and stretch her legs in the airport before she would get on the road. A server found an empty table for Jackie at Obrycki's, and she sat down.

A crab cake will be perfect, she thought.

She wished she could drink a beer but did not think it would be a good idea with having to meet with Helga afterward, so she settled for an iced tea.

Jackie devoured the crab cake and the fries so fast she gave herself a stomachache.

It was delicious, she admitted to herself.

She always seemed to eat too quickly when she was overtired.

She headed for the baggage area to see her bag, the only one left, circling around the carousel. She then headed to her car and drove to the office as ordered.

Scanning in her card at security, Jackie stopped to chat with Mark a little before an urgent Helga interrupted her.

"Please follow me," she said.

Jackie followed her into a conference room she had never been in before. At the long table on a corner sat a burly man with some equipment he was tinkering with. Helga indicated her to sit in the chair opposite this man on the corner and disappeared out the door.

To her amazement, she realized she was about to be poly-graphed. Not knowing why, she was a little nervous. Or this was just the way they worked here, and from time to time, you had a surprise test. She forced herself to calm down. She had nothing to hide.

The polygraph man began.

"Hello, I am Brian Hill. I will be doing your polygraph test. You are Jackie Ford, correct?"

Jackie nodded.

"I will ask you a series of questions and will need you to reply with a yes or a no. Nothing else. Understand?"

"Yes," replied Jackie.

Brian attached the straps and finger detection probes and began.

"Are you Jackie Ford?"

"Yes."

"Are you Caron Tucker?"

"Yes."

"Are you from Baltimore?"

"Yes."

"Do you own a house in Baltimore?"

"No."

"Did you just fly in from Canada?"

"No."

"Did you tell anyone any details of your assignments?"

"No."

"Are you in contact with any ex-employees of this agency?"

"No."

"Have you offered protection assistance to anyone outside this agency?"

"No."

"Have you ever killed anyone?"

"Yes."

"Have you ever killed anyone outside of your job requirements?"

"No."

"Have you left any task information in a place where it could be viewed by others?"

"No."

"Have you ever helped someone by giving them unimportant details from your assignment?"

"No."

"Have you ever done anything in any capacity to compromise the security or identity of the agency?"

"No."

"Okay, that will be all, Ms. Ford. You may return to Helga's office."

Brian ripped the paper off the machine and walked with Jackie to Helga's office.

"She is not your leak," he said and exited.

Jackie felt relieved, not understanding fully what this was about.

Helga said, "Here is your next assignment. Please read it in your car." She handed the envelope to Jackie. "You are dismissed."

Jackie's new instructions read: "Drive your car to Pittsburgh where you will check in to the DoubleTree downtown on Bigelow Square."

Ugh, she thought.

Jackie was not up for a four-hour drive or better, depending on traffic. She would wait until she got to Pittsburgh to read the details and get the drive over with.

She wondered what was going on that warranted the polygraph test. The questions gave some insight. Someone must have given an assignment detail to someone they should not have. It was not her, so she dismissed that concern and set her GPS for Pittsburgh.

She was happy and grateful she still had the Porsche to drive. The Pennsylvania Turnpike was a boring, monotonous road. Jackie would make it fun. She once again blasted her music and cruised down the road singing.

Winding her way into downtown and just past PPG Paints Arena, Jackie found the hotel for this assignment. She took advantage of the handicapped spot again without guilt. She went to her room to find the details of her next assignment.

Jackie was getting into the routine of the job, always a room with details in the envelope and supplies. She opened the envelope to reveal her next task, and a ticket fell onto the floor: a Penguins versus Capitals game ticket dated for tomorrow at 1:00 p.m.

Jackie looked at the paper and read:

> Target—Igor Strostanovich, Penguins hockey player
>
> Location—PPG Stadium and Dream Weavers Day Spa
>
> Your identification—Caitlyn Moore. See driver's license picture for reference on makeup.
>
> Target is a Russian-born player for the Pittsburgh Penguins. He has an appointment for the Dream Weavers Day Spa Saturday after the game at 8:00 p.m. where he tends to entertain hookers.
>
> Find the vulnerable point and eliminate the target. Once the task is completed, immediately return to the Baltimore Hilton by car.
>
> You will be bringing all weapons back as well, leaving the room empty of any supplies. You will find your Baltimore hotel room key in your app upon return.
>
> Be smart.
>
> Be safe.

Jackie saw a small firearm with the silencer on the desk alongside a knife in a sheath. There was a concealed carry holster for inside her jacket.

She tried the holster on and adjusted it to fit tightly against her body. Jackie already knew the task would have to be completed between the stadium and spa or at the spa itself. She would not be able to sneak a gun into a stadium and did not want to even attempt that.

She looked at the clothes and saw a bathing suit and some very revealing clothing. They must be for the spa if she wanted to complete her task there.

She also saw Penguins gear and laughed that she would have to wear that coming from Washington Caps territory.

Jackie chose a dress, flats, and the jacket and headed to the spa on the other side of the arena. She would check out the way people came and went, get the lay of the land. Along the way, she looked for vulnerabilities, but with the number of people on the street, she thought she was reduced to the spa option.

She walked the long way back to the hotel and found a pizza place that looked good to get her dinner. She ordered pizza and beer to go and headed back to her hotel. This stay would be a short one.

Jackie downed the beer and hardly touched her pizza and crawled into bed, feeling drained. Her second wind had come to an absolute halt. She flipped on the TV for background noise and left it playing a random movie while she dozed off to sleep.

CHAPTER 53

Jackie put on the Penguins gear and a pair of jeans and walked to the game. Her hair was still very dark, and when she caught her reflection in the windows she passed, she felt anonymous. She had never been to a hockey game and was interested in the experience.

She easily found her seat a couple of rows off the glass near the Penguins box. It allowed her to get a good look at her target ahead of time. Yes, she had the photos Helga always provided, but this was helpful too.

She cheered when others cheered and booed when others booed. Jackie acted the part of a Penguins fan as she watched them lose to the Capitals. Somehow, this made her smile inside. She was not a fan per se, but it was her home team in her eyes, so winning was great, especially in an away game.

Jackie exited back up the steps, appearing to be pouting, and headed to the hotel.

Now for the tricky part, she thought.

Jackie put on the bright-pink bikini and covered it with a jean skirt and a cropped top with slits down her arms.

She also had platform heels she put on to her dismay. If she had to run, it would not be so easy. She put her hair up in a messy bun on top of her head and added makeup to her eyes to look excessive and cheap like her identification.

The gun seemed more concealed in pieces in the jacket pockets, so she went with that. She popped a couple of pieces of bubble gum in her mouth and chomped on them as she walked out of her room and headed to the spa.

Jackie arrived fifteen minutes ahead of Igor's appointment and spoke in a hushed tone to the counter help.

"I'm here for Igor. He here yet?" she said and popped her bubble gum, totally portraying the stereotypical streetwalker.

"Not yet," replied the young lady, smiling.

"Can I get back to his room to wait?" asked Jackie. "He has a room or something, right?"

"He usually rents out the entire spa and the pool," she replied. "Go ahead back. Second door on the left is the ladies' locker room. You will see signs for the entrance door to the pool. You can wait in the pool area for him."

Jackie slipped into the locker room as directed and continued straight to the pool area. From there, she found the men's room and entered, ignoring the receptionist's instruction. Luckily, her target had rented out the entire place, so no one would be in the locker room.

She didn't have much time before Igor's arrival, so she took off her blouse to reveal the pink bikini top, laid her top with her jacket on a bench nearest the pool door, and put the gun in a towel. She carried the towel rolled up under her arm and walked toward the door just as it swung open.

Igor entered.

"Well, hello there." Igor smiled.

"Hello yourself, sweet thing," replied Jackie, grinning and popping her gum again. "Come on and sit down here and let sugar take real good care of you."

Eager for the care, Igor did as he was instructed.

Jackie began to rub one shoulder and whispered, "Does this feel good, big daddy?" and, with the other hand, squeezed off a round into Igor's temple.

She grabbed her shirt and jacket and raced out through the pool and into the ladies' room. There, she put her top and jacket back on, took the silencer off, and stuffed both the pieces of her weapon into separate pockets.

Jackie walked quickly to the front door, hearing the receptionist yell after her, "He just went back."

She continued out the door and walked very quickly back to the hotel garage and her car. She slowed to a saunter as she entered the garage, seeing another car exiting and not wishing to draw unwanted attention.

Finally reaching the car, she pulled a sweatshirt out from the bag she had the forethought to pack and slipped it over her outfit. She then used a hotel room makeup remover towelette to get rid of the atrocious look, and she let her hair out of the messy bun.

Jackie was out of the garage two minutes later. There was no alarm noted and no police, so Jackie carefully drove until she was up on the highway.

She pushed the talk button on her phone and said, "Call Helga" then heard the familiar double ring.

Helga answered with a yes.

"Task is completed," said Jackie.

Helga grunted in affirmation and hung up the phone.

Roaring down the Pennsylvania Turnpike on her way back to Baltimore, Jackie did not care if she got pulled over. She felt invincible. She thought of her past and wished another douche would try to hurt her in some way.

What Jackie mostly enjoyed was the power of ability.

And able she certainly proved to be in a brief period, she thought.

But really it was not so short a period. Jackie had been training for years before this job.

She flipped on the radio and pressed the command button.

"Play Queens of the Stone Age on Spotify," she said.

The music played.

We get some rules to follow...

And Jackie joined in.

That and this / These and those / No one knows.

This might be Jackie's favorite band. At least it was this very moment.

CHAPTER 54

Allison was enjoying her downtime, having purchased a book to keep her company. She was reading it now when she heard the ping of a text and looked at her phone. Helga requested she come to the office immediately. She set the book aside and put on her shoes and left.

When she arrived at the office, she was escorted to the conference room where the same man who polygraphed Jackie sat. He introduced himself and got right into the questions.

"Are you Allison Kincaid?"

"Yes."

"Are you Shelly Carson?"

"Yes."

"Are you from Baltimore?"

"Yes."

"Do you own a house in Baltimore?"

"No."

"Did you just fly in from Canada?"

"No."

"Did you tell anyone any details of your assignments?"

"No."

"Are you in contact with any ex-employees of this agency?"

"No."

"Have you offered protection assistance to anyone outside this agency?"

"No."

"Have you ever killed anyone?"

"Yes."

"Have you ever killed anyone outside of your job requirements?"

"No."

"Have you left any task information in a place where it could be viewed by others?"

"No."

"Have you ever helped someone by giving them unimportant details from your assignment?"

"No."

"Have you ever done anything in any capacity to compromise the security or identity of the agency?"

"No."

"Okay. Please remain here until I return."

Brian once again ripped the paper off the machine, but this time, he walked alone to Helga's office.

"She is inconclusive. I am leaning toward truth, but the question regarding sharing any unimportant details, she answered falsely. I am thinking she may have made a general statement of sorts but no details about an assignment," he said and exited.

Helga considered the information and decided to send Allison on her next assignment, but she would pay close attention to this asset for now. Brian returned to the room and told Allison she may go to Helga's office. Nervous about the situation, Allison did as instructed and sat in the chair opposite of Helga.

Helga spoke, "I will have your next assignment sent to the hotel. You may return there now. You are dismissed."

Allison left, though with a troubled feeling in her gut. Something did not feel right about this sudden polygraph test.

Later at the hotel, Allison heard a tapping at her door and peeped out the hole. There was an older man with the now recognizable envelope and suitcase. She took both and sat back on her bed and read her next assignment.

It seemed assignments were never-ending now, and she barely had downtime these days. She ripped open the envelope to see what the next adventure was to be.

Target—Jeremy Anderson

Location—London, England

Your identification—Caroline Moore.

Use the wig provided and contacts to change your eyes to bright blue.

Your flight leaves BWI Airport to Heathrow at 10:00 p.m. tonight.

Your return flight is Wednesday at 11:15 p.m.

Once you arrive at Heathrow, take a taxi to the Hilton London Syon Park. Your app will have your room key.

Target will be playing tennis at the All England Lawn Tennis and Croquet Club in Wimbledon Park on number two court Wednesday evening at six thirty. When done, he will go for a run up Church Street and into the park toward the lake then circle back.

Find the best advantage location and complete your task.

Be smart.

Be safe.

Oh no, she thought, *not another assignment in a park.*
Allison looked at the photos of her target and was shocked to see it was a young teenager, fourteen years old at best. How could this boy be a terrorist? Or a threat to the US or their ally, the UK?

She did not think she could do this one. It just seemed wrong. Maybe there was misunderstanding for this task. She phoned Helga for clarity.

"Yes?" answered Helga.

"It's Allison. I have questions on this assignment." She got straight to the issue. "Maybe I misunderstood that this was to be an assassination. What is this kid involved in that made him a target?"

Helga responded, "You do not get the particulars, just the assignment to complete. You must trust that he is a necessary target. All your assignments require this. You know this, Allison."

Allison was still weary and said, "I'd like to reject this assignment, please. I do not believe I can complete it. He's just a boy, and I can't seem to wrap my head around taking his life."

Helga responded, "That is your choice, of course," and hung up the phone.

Relieved she would not have a young boy's blood on her hands, she packed the task back into the suitcase. She supposed she would have to wait for the next assignment to show up at her door.

Allison decided to go down to the lobby bar for a drink. She would look to see if there was someone to chat with. As she approached the bar, she saw a very good-looking man drinking a frosty mug of beer. She slid into the seat next to him and said hello. He smiled and put his hand out in introduction.

"I'm Brady."

"I'm Allison."

She turned to the bar and ordered herself a beer too.

"A little day drinking, Brady?"

"A little boredom drinking," he replied and laughed.

"Same," said Allison. "Traveling?" she continued.

"I am. I am from Santa Fe. Here one more day on business. You?" asked Brady.

"Again, same." She laughed.

Allison noted the wedding band on his left ring finger but did not care. She wanted human touch. This would be safe, as he would most certainly would want her to disappear later, which of course worked perfectly for her.

A few drinks in, they decided to order a fourth to carry to Brady's room. As soon as they closed the door, Allison began removing her clothes. She saw the delight in Brady's eyes as he lounged back to watch her progression to nakedness.

Allison watched his eyes trail over her well-trained body and enjoyed the pleased expression from Brady. As she approached the bed, Brady disrobed quickly and scooped her up then laid her on the bed.

He began kissing her stomach and wandered south, to Allison's delight. She enjoyed the slow motion of his mouth and then the quick insertion into her once she was very wet. Allison let out a quiet moan of approval.

CHAPTER 55

Later that evening, as Allison lay back in her bed, she heard that soft tap at her door and knew her next assignment was here. She peeped out to see the same man and the same suitcase and envelope as always. Hopefully, this target would not be too hard for her. She exchanged suitcases and envelopes.

She sat on her bed and tore open the new envelope.

> Target—Emanuel Calli. You should know this time he is a drug cartel kingpin, and you need to be aware of his protection units.
>
> Location—Tijuana, Mexico
>
> Your identification—Emily Hale, no alteration necessary.
>
> Your flight leaves on Friday at 7:30 p.m. from BWI.
>
> Your return flight will be determined upon completion of task.
>
> Take the shuttle from Tijuana Airport to the Hampton Inn. Your app will have the room key.
>
> Target will be playing golf at Campo de Golf Club Campestre, Tijuana on Saturday at 8:00

a.m. and Sunday at 8:00 a.m. You will determine the best way to eliminate this target.

Sunday will be the last day you will have an opportunity to complete this assignment.

Be smart.

Be safe.

At least Helga let her know it would be another drug kingpin. Allison opened her suitcase to find minimal clothing—shorts, shirts, sandals, and golf shoes.

Her passport showed a picture of herself with her name changed. Allison found it curious and was disappointed to not have a disguise for this task but did not put much more thought into it as she gathered her bathroom items to add to the suitcase. Short on time, she hurried out to her car and headed to catch her flight.

CHAPTER 56

Jackie stopped by to pick up an order of Bubba Gump's gumbo and biscuits on her way to the hotel. She fully intended to eat the big meal so that she could drink an excessive amount of alcohol. She felt the need to celebrate.

The celebratory mood felt odd for a second, but she pushed away the feeling, knowing she was a queen. She believed she was incredibly good at her job. Nobody would ever suspect she had done the Russian terrorist in. Ever.

She laughed a euphoric laugh again and parked her Porsche in the same handicapped spot. Jackie stopped by the bar in the hotel lobby and ordered three bottles of Guinness to take to her room. Exiting the elevator onto her floor, she saw the woman with the envelope at her door about to knock.

Jackie's elation died. She was not to get a break this time either. No Guinness and no hot bath it would seem. She exchanged suitcases, took the envelope, and entered her room.

I will eat before I read this at the very least, she thought.

She switched on the TV and opened the container of gumbo. She leisurely ate and drank down a beer before looking at the contents of the envelope.

Jackie sobered immediately. She stared in disbelief at the assignment written on this paper. By this time, Jackie had settled into her job and never thought twice about the assignments she was given. But this one?

She was completely torn and scared and worried. Emotions ran the gamut and ended in panic. She picked up the paper to read the task again, and as she did, her phone rang. It was Helga. Jackie let it ring a few times before answering, knowing she could not ignore Helga.

"Hello," she said.

Helga, in a very stern voice, asked in a demanding way, "You will not have trouble fulfilling your task, yes?"

Jackie instinctively knew she should answer affirmatively.

"No problem at all. I'm sure there is a valid reason for this."

Helga responded, "There is. This will be the one time I give an explanation for obvious reasons. Your target is threatening to reveal our organization's covert operations unless we pay her a five-million-dollar extortion. We at the agency were shocked at this turn of events and are saddened that this issue did arise. We do not take the handing out this assignment lightly, I assure you. As you know, we had all the assets take a polygraph test. Your target failed hers."

Jackie felt better with the revelation.

"I see. That is indeed a very troubling issue. I will do what is necessary. Our identity will not be compromised, I promise," she said and hung up the phone.

Still, there was a twinge of worry.

"It is my job to protect the US government," she assured herself. She read the paper a third time.

Target—Shelly Carson, alias Allison Kincaid, alias Emily Hale

Location—Tijuana, Mexico

Flight leaves BWI at 9:02 p.m.

Return flight leaves Tijuana at 10:12 a.m.

Upon arrival at the Tijuana Airport, take a cab to the Hampton Inn. Be very aware, as target is staying in room 327. Your room is 227 and will be accessible by app as always.

Your identification—Merissa Lopez. There is a wig for your disguise. Otherwise there are no further required alterations.

Target will be scoping out the Campo de Golf Club Campestre, Tijuana at approximately 7:00 a.m. Her intended target will be golfing at 8:00 a.m., so the task will need to be completed before then.

Additional details—There is a connecting staircase between the floors just outside your room. We will need a picture taken and texted upon completion of this assignment.

Be smart.

Be safe.

Jackie opened the suitcase and pulled out a wig of short red hair with the tips dyed back. She tried it on and felt it was a great, easy disguise. She looked at her watch and saw she had a few hours to make her flight. She downed another beer and hopped in the shower. She would need to have nerves of steel to complete this task.

CHAPTER 57

Jackie's flight was running behind by half an hour. It was adding stress to an already stressful situation. Her time on the other end would be extremely limited to complete this task. As her flight descended into Tijuana, she began to develop alternate plans in her head just in case she had to act immediately upon arrival.

Exiting the airport, she saw the shuttle for the Hampton Inn about to leave. She waved it down and jumped on, figuring it would be quicker than a cab.

The shuttle dropped her at the hotel, and she walked very quickly to the stairway, deciding not to chance an encounter in the elevator. She noiselessly slipped into her room and began preparations to kill Allison.

On the desk lay a key card to Allison's room, a knife in a sheath, and a 9 mm semiautomatic handgun with a silencer. Jackie decided to have both weapons with her, as her target was no ordinary target. Allison was every bit as lethal as she was, and Jackie knew that if she did not act quickly and decisively, she could lose her own life.

Jackie sat down to study the map of the area and put a plan together. She did not have the advantage of scoping the area of the golf course, as Allison would be sure to recognize her. This was not going to be easy.

Jackie reconsidered the room key and thought she should do this now. Allison should be sleeping, getting the little rest available before the morning dawned. Taking a deep breath to calm her nerves, Jackie jumped into action.

Quietly, she exited her room and crept up the stairs to the floor above. The stairway door to the third floor creaked a bit as she pushed it open but not too loudly.

Inside her room, Allison heard the creak from the hallway and grabbed her gun just in case; she still had that gnawing feeling in her gut. She was fully awake and had been having a tough time falling asleep, as the town was extremely noisy and the polygraph had messed with her head.

Allison knew she was correct in worrying when the door to her room clicked and quietly opened. Standing in the closet behind the door, she watched Jackie enter. She thought it could be Jackie, but no way she would do this.

No way the agency would send Jackie whom she could identify immediately. Was this a sick, twisted perversion from Helga? She had to know, so Allison flipped on the light and said, "Stop and keep your hands where I can see them."

Jackie turned to face her. Allison could not prevent the tears that flowed.

"How could you do this, Jackie?" she asked.

Jackie replied, "How could you extort the agency and threaten to reveal their true purpose?"

"So that is what they told you. Come on, Jackie. Think for yourself. They had to give you a story because they knew you would not do this otherwise. Here is the real story: I declined to kill a young boy. He was barely a teenager. I dared to question the almighty Helga. She pretended to understand and gave me a new assignment. I am going to guess now that the new assignment was bogus to get me here in an area of high crime. That would make it easy to explain. Tourist killed while visiting Tijuana. Everyone would agree what a shame it was but the area. She should have known better."

Jackie felt confused.

"Why would the agency do this? They say you failed your polygraph," Jackie asked.

She did not yet understand. What was clear to Jackie was that she had to make a quick decision because now her life would be in jeopardy if she did not complete this task.

"I don't believe you. Why should I believe you?"

Allison replied, "Because don't you think I would have shot you by now if it weren't true? I have you at the disadvantage. I am fairly sure I failed the polygraph because they asked a question about telling anyone any details of an assignment, and I said no. But we both know I told you I was headed to LA to protect the children of actors."

Jackie slowly lowered her weapon as tears began to stream down her face too. Shocked, she almost made the greatest mistake of her life. Jackie walked over and sat on the bed. Allison sat next to her.

"Oh my God. Now what do we do?" she said.

CHAPTER 58

"Fake your death," Jackie blurted. "That is the only other option, or there will be others after us both. Hopefully that will keep them at bay for now. Let's look and see if there are any costumes stores nearby."

Both women picked up their phones and googled for costume stores and theatrical makeup stores in the area. They found a few, but none of them opened until at least 10:00 a.m. That would be too late.

They randomly chose a costume store and decided to break in and get the things needed to make a gunshot kill look authentic. At 3:30 a.m., the alarm that rang sounded extremely loud, so they hastily found what they needed and ran behind the store across the street and then back to the hotel.

It was almost 5:00 a.m., so they needed to act quickly. Allison lay on the bed as though shot in her sleep, and Jackie poured the fake blood next to her head on the bed. Next she attached a bullet wound and carefully faded the area to look bruised to create an entry wound.

Jackie then took a pillow and shot a hole through it. She placed the pillow on the bed above Allison's head as though she had removed it after the kill. Next she took photos in low light to capture the kill in the most authentic way possible.

She selected one and texted it to Helga and said, "Target eliminated."

It was now 6:15 a.m. Relieved to be done with this part of the farse, they cleaned up, and Jackie ran down to get some breakfast for them both.

"So now what?" asked Allison as she ate the biscuit Jackie had brought back to the room.

Jackie shrugged. "Good question. Somehow you need to return to the US. You could walk across the border then find a ride. Get back to the east coast. Let's buy burner phones so that we can talk and not be traced. When you get back to Baltimore, I will stow you in my room until we can figure out this mess."

"What about the old boxing gym I used to hide out in?" asked Allison.

"That I do not recommend. You would be involving those people too," Jackie said. "Let us think this through. We have some time before you are back. I need to go. My flight is in a couple hours, and it would not be good to miss this one," said Jackie as she hugged Allison goodbye. "Be smart, be safe," she said with a wink.

CHAPTER 59

Jackie slid into her first-class seat with a sigh. She checked her phone as always and saw there was a message from Helga: "Return to the office for a debriefing at 7:00 a.m." Of course Helga would want to make sure she did not go off the deep end after this assignment.

Jackie ordered a drink and put her music in her ears.

No Queens this time, she thought, feeling incredibly low.

She chose her playlist of sad love songs and settled into the first song, Christina Perri's "Jar of Hearts." The ride home would feel terribly long.

Jackie pulled into her same handicapped space at the agency and, for the first time, felt a twinge of guilt. She entered the building, careful to keep a stoic look on her face.

The assignment was just another assignment, she told herself.

She rounded the corner to Helga's office and entered the open door.

"Sit," said Helga.

Jackie chose the chair on the right and sat.

"Good morning. How was your assignment?" asked Helga.

"It was an important assignment for me. Threatening this agency and exposing our program would have been a huge blow to our national security. I fully understood the necessity."

"Excellent," said Helga. "Follow me."

Helga got up, and Jackie followed her down the hall to the director's office. Director Franklin rose to greet her.

"Jackie, you are an unsung national hero. I wanted to personally thank you for effectively eliminating a significant threat to our integrity as a country."

"Yes, sir," replied Jackie.

As the director sat back down, she noticed a list on a corkboard next to his desk. It had a lot of numbers under the asset column and color coded-entries under the outcome column. Many were notations that looked to be red *T*s.

"I won't keep you. I just wanted to extend my gratitude. It's assets like you that keep the world safe and terrorists at bay."

Jackie nodded.

The director then asked, "How do you like the Porsche?"

Jackie responded, "I love the car and am very appreciative you allow me to drive it."

"I think you have earned it. The car is now yours."

Jackie looked into his eyes and smiled. "Thank you. That is very generous of you."

"Keep up the good work, Ford. You have a bright future here at the agency," said the director.

He waved his hand for dismissal, and Helga tugged Jackie's arm to exit.

Back in Helga's office, she continued, "You have also earned a vacation. Do you have a preference?"

Jackie again smiled and promptly chose the Outer Banks of North Carolina.

"Very well," said Helga. "I will send you a confirmation of your accommodations. You are dismissed."

Jackie chose the location because she knew Allison was en route to the east coast. She would check in with her later outside of the car in case it was bugged.

By the time Jackie arrived back at the hotel, her arrangements were in her messages:

Location—1716 Fifth Avenue, Duck, NC

This is a waterfront house rented beginning tomorrow. All clothes and beach needs will be provided on premises. You may fly and rent a car or drive to the location. Your choice.

The car, duh, she thought.

So this could work out to be perfect, thought Jackie.

She left her work phone in her room and exited to call Allison from outside. Allison had made it to Oklahoma already, hitching with truck drivers.

Smart, thought Jackie.

She would continue hitching, and Jackie would touch base tomorrow on her way to the Outer Banks.

CHAPTER 60

Jackie packed up her few belongings and decided to head to Annapolis. She had a plan formulated in her head. She wanted to check out boat rentals and get crabs at Buddy's since she was going to be near the restaurant.

She pulled into the boat rental company and entered the office to inquire about their list of available boats. She checked off the ones that had to be captained and found one she wanted to do a long-term lease on and dialed Helga's number.

"Hi, Helga. I was wondering about renting a boat in Annapolis. Maybe it could be my home base for the summer instead of the Hilton?"

Helga's red flags went up.

"Oh?" she replied.

"I've always wanted a boat, but it seems renting is better than buying these days," said Jackie.

Helga replied, "I will have to check with the director for approval. Can you have the contract faxed to our offices?"

"Of course. Thank you for considering this," Jackie replied.

Helga hung up the phone and immediately walked to Jack's office.

"We may have a problem, sir."

She went on and explained the circumstances of Jackie's request to rent a boat for the summer.

"Go ahead and grant permission. But get eyes on her and extra eyes on that boat as soon as she arrives back from vacation."

Helga signed the document, added the financial information, and faxed it back while Jackie was still there. To Jackie's surprise and delight, she would now call a fifty-four-foot Silverton yacht called Sea Beast home for the summer.

Jackie boarded the Sea Beast to investigate the interior.

This is perfect, she thought.

She left her phone on the galley's countertop and stepped on to the deck to call Allison and give her the news. Allison would come to the boat instead of the hotel.

She found the captain and handed him five one-hundred-dollar bills.

"I need you to be discreet. If someone questions you about me, tell them I am always alone. There will be a woman here within a couple days. This is her picture."

Jackie showed a picture of Allison to the captain.

"She is hiding here to escape an abusive husband with connections to bad people. Keep the boat away from the dock when I am not here. If anyone requests to board, please deny access. I will call you before my expected arrival to board with the next time being in a week. I only have this cash on me now, but I will have more and will compensate you better than you could imagine. Are you the right man for the job?"

Matt nodded, a bit bewildered. Nothing like this had ever happened to him before.

"I think I can do this," he said.

Jackie thought his tall, muscular frame would be a deterrent, at least a little, if someone tried to access the boat.

Stepping back on to the dock, Jackie headed to Buddy's for the crabs. She finished off a dozen and more than a few beers before she stumbled back to the boat. She would leave in the morning for Duck.

When Jackie woke the next morning, they were anchored off the dock but still near the harbor. She had slept soundly with the gentle movement of the water.

She found Matt on deck drinking a cup of coffee and eating a bagel. He motioned toward the galley.

"There's more coffee and bagels if you like."

Jackie did like and retreated to get both.

She returned and said good morning. Matt smiled in response.

"Can you take me out on the bay for a couple hours?"

"It would be my pleasure," he replied.

Matt jumped into the captain's seat, started the motor, and pulled the anchors up. He very slowly exited the harbor and onto the Severn River. The Naval Academy looked stately from the river as they passed by.

Now entering the Chesapeake Bay and to her left, Jackie could see the Bay Bridge and the choppy water beneath. They cruised in that direction, and Jackie found herself under the bridge looking up at the cars that were traveling over.

She saw a dozen or so center console boats anchored to fish in the area, and she watched as an angler pulled a big catfish out as they passed by. Once in the channel, Matt sped up.

Jackie came over and sat on the seat next to Matt as he pointed out things.

"To our right is Kent Island."

Of course, thought Jackie.

She knew it was right over the Bay Bridge.

"To our left coming up is the Magothy River and then Gibson Island. Right behind Gibson Island is a small place called Dobbin Island where many boats drop anchor and party all day."

He pointed toward the water.

"All those bobbing floats in the water have crab traps attached to them below. We steer clear of those."

Matt had a narration for most of the area. They soon passed the Patapsco River and saw the Key Bridge.

"Hart Miller Island over there is another party spot on the bay. It's much bigger and closer to Baltimore, so it attracts many more boats."

"We should turn back," said Jackie. "I need to drive to the Outer Banks today."

Matt spun the boat around and headed back south toward Annapolis. Jackie took the moment to relax and further consider her plan of getting Allison to safety.

She knew she would ask Matt to do things he might be uncomfortable with and left him with an additional two thousand dollars to hopefully make it worth his while. They exchanged phone numbers before Jackie stepped off the boat so that Matt could be alerted to Allison's arrival as well as her own return.

CHAPTER 61

Back behind the wheel of the Porsche, Jackie allowed herself to enjoy the car again.

"I can't always be down," she reasoned.

She blasted music once again and rolled her windows all the way down.

A couple of hours into the drive, Jackie pulled into a Wendy's restaurant off the Ashland exit of 95 south to get some lunch. The bagel would only get her so far. She ordered a chicken sandwich and an iced tea and ate in her car.

She tried to think about her next moves with Allison but was not focused. She needed to not drink excessively and keep a clear head until she had a concrete plan in place. She decided to use the rest of the drive to think.

Finishing up the chicken, Jackie noticed a black BMW sitting at the back of the lot.

Could it be the one I have been traveling with on 95? He did stay with me like cars are apt to do when traveling long distances. Am I getting paranoid?

She left her work phone in the car and walked back into Wendy's to use the restroom. There she called Allison and voiced her suspicions. The boat must have caused concern. They agreed. Allison would have to be super careful boarding.

Jackie gave her Matt's phone number and said to give him a call for help getting on the boat. Allison was now in Virginia and soon would be at the docks. She decided to call Matt immediately and make the arrangement.

Jackie strode back to her car a few minutes later, making sure the black BMW saw her throw a paper towel in a trash can. She got in the car and roared back onto the interstate, noting the BMW creeping out too. For now, Jackie was unconcerned, as this part of the trip would genuinely be a vacation and there would be no news to report back to Helga or the director.

Jackie found the rental house just as the sun was setting. She parked under the house and entered with the keypad number provided. She climbed the steps to the first floor and investigated. It had three bedrooms, all with their own bathrooms.

She settled on the one where they had already placed some clothes for her and dropped her bag of her toiletries in the bathroom. She headed up the second flight of stairs to the top floor. It had a kitchen, dining area, and family room with a huge TV and fireplace.

She opened the blinds to a deck that ran the length of the house and slid the door open. It overlooked the ocean, and she let the peace wash over her, as it always does when she is near the ocean.

Leaving the door open, she walked to the refrigerator and opened the door.

Yes, Guinness! They are really getting to know the details of my tastes at the agency, she thought.

She reached in for a cold bottle and relaxed on the deck in the waning light until it was very dark.

She could hear young lovers on the beach below her deck and smiled. Obviously, they were unaware of her presence. Jackie felt that twinge of loneliness as she listened, secretly invading their privacy but unable to pull herself away.

She watched the shadows of the young lovers stroll away toward the north hand in hand. Jackie went inside and grabbed a pillow and throw from the family room and made a bed on the deck for the night. She would enjoy this vacation fully because in her gut, she knew the shit was about to hit the fan.

CHAPTER 62

Allison called Matt and explained that she was the woman coming to stay on the boat. Matt, who wanted to be helpful, offered the girlfriend angle as a cover. Allison would disguise herself as best as possible, and Matt would greet her as though she were his girlfriend.

And so Matt was sitting on the deck with the boat tied up in dock when Allison found the Sea Beast and yelled up to him, "Matt! I'm here!"

Matt yelled, "Coming, love!" and jumped down to help her aboard.

He embraced and kissed her like a girlfriend and gave her a seat. He untied the boat and set off to the bay. Once they were away from others and out on the bay, they spoke.

"I'm sorry you are in such an ugly situation, but I am here to help in any way if I can," Matt began.

"Thank you," Allison replied, relaxing into a cushy chair behind Matt.

"I believe you were undetected," he said. "I didn't see anyone hanging around for a while and watching."

Allison had to agree.

She had not noticed anyone following her at all. Of course, the agency thought she was dead, so she did have that advantage. She sent off a text to Jackie that said "Arrived safely."

They were, in fact, not detected. Helga and her henchman were focusing on Jackie until she returned. Matt and Allison would have a worry-free week ahead of them.

Matt navigated the boat all the way down to the Cambridge city docks. He tied up and set out to find supplies. They would need food and gas if they were to spend the week on the bay. Allison's only request was a bikini. She was looking forward to genuinely relaxing and soaking up some sunshine.

CHAPTER 63

Jackie put on one of the bikinis she found in a drawer and a pretty white lacy cover-up. In her beach bag, she dumped a book, some sunscreen, a towel, and a couple of Guinness. She grabbed a chair and headed down to the beach.

She had brought *Anna Karenina* by Leo Tolstoy with her, her perennial favorite. She opened the new copy, having had to get rid of her worn copy with this job, and began reading the lament of the opening pages. She was entranced with the story despite knowing she was being watched by the agency.

Jackie continued her boring routine for the entirety of her vacation before heading back to reality. She gave her shadow absolutely nothing to report to Helga and, hopefully, quieting any suspicions they might have had.

*****

Matt eased the Sea Beast carefully up to the dock in Annapolis. He and Allison had had a fun week on the bay. Matt fished some and would cook for dinner whatever he reeled in each day. Allison laid on the deck, tanning and drinking the beer Matt had bought on his stop in Cambridge.

Music was always playing. Matt asked little about Allison's situation, and she offered no details. They kept it light the entire week, laughing at songs they both messed up singing when they had too much to drink or working together to free a well-embedded anchor.

Jackie had returned from vacation and was pulling into the parking lot of the marina near the Annapolis dock. She rolled her suitcase over the brick road and hopped aboard the boat. She sent off a text to Helga to inform her she was now on the boat, safely returned home from vacation. Although she was sure it had already been confirmed by her shadow.

Part of her was glad to be back, and part of her was nervous for the double life she would now live. She and Matt sat on deck to give the "eyes" more fodder to pass on to Helga. After a drink and a snack, Matt started the motors and pulled the anchors to head out.

Jackie displayed herself up front like a figurehead of old-time vessels. They slowly pulled away and then down the Severn River as they had on their last voyage. Once safely out of sight, she went to get Allison.

Hugging then sitting, they began to chatter. After the pleasantries, Jackie got down to business.

"What do you think the plan should be?" she asked.

Allison looked serious.

"We have to figure out why it was so important to get rid of me. I do not believe I know anything harmful about the agency, but they are clearly worried about me. That is what we need to figure out. I am sure the entire world knows that covert anti-terrorist efforts exist within our government. But the hit on me does not make sense. I do know that the director, Jack Franklin, keeps files on us. I saw this when I was in his office a few weeks ago. Maybe we can access those files and see if we can dig up the dirt we need?"

"That won't be easy. There is someone manning the door 24-7," said Jackie.

They both retreated into their thoughts, searching for the solution to obtaining the files in Helga's and the director's offices.

CHAPTER 66

"Let us go over this plan one last time," said Jackie.

"Okay," started Allison. "You drop me off a block south of the office then continue on to the agency and park in your handicapped space as usual. I run to the building and approach from behind, shoot out the two security cameras so they cannot catch my likeness on tape. You enter with your credentials through the front of the building and speak to the security guard, exchange niceties until you notice the back cameras are out on his monitors."

"Meanwhile," Allison continued. "I will be breaking into a window in Helga's office. The alarm will sound. The security guard will react, and you pretend to join him in the investigation into where the break-in occurred. You tell him to take the director's office while you check Helga's office. You exit Helga's office and quickly come up behind the security guard and subdue him with the stun gun. You tie him up and go back to shut the alarm system down. At this point, we figure that Helga and the director have already received alerts that the offices had a break-in. You scour the files in the director's office, and I scour Helga's and grab what we can and exit to your car. We head back to the boat that Matt will have docked at the inner harbor. We will head down the Patapsco River to the bay and take it all the way out on the ocean."

"Perfect," replied Jackie.

"Perfect," agreed Matt.

"Thank you, Jackie. I know that you will no longer be an asset for the agency after you do this."

Jackie nodded. What else could she do? She no longer wanted this job anyway. Not after what she had been asked to do to Allison.

CHAPTER 67

With night approaching, Matt pulled the Sea Beast into the docks of the inner harbor. Jackie was waiting in her car half a block away for Allison to join her. They headed to Patterson Avenue and the place where this whole crazy saga had begun to put their plan in motion.

As Allison hopped out of the car, she said sarcastically, "Be smart. Be safe," and closed the car door behind her. Before Jackie could get the car back on the road, Allison was already running. She drove past Allison, turned into the lot, and swung right into her parking spot.

Jackie was very anxious but determined. She had to deliberately calm her nerves, as she knew what she was about to set in motion. She may never be safe again in her lifetime.

She scanned her card to let herself in and spoke to the guard.

"Hi, Mark, I didn't know you worked nights."

"Yep, sometimes I do. Why are you here so late yourself?"

And as they had perfectly timed, the alarm sounded, then Mark saw the cameras were down.

Following the plan, Jackie pulled out her weapon and said, "Check the director's area. I'll start with Helga's."

Mark nodded and proceeded as directed. Moments later, Mark felt the burn and collapsed. He realized that Jackie was tying him up.

How stupid was I? he thought.

He had a crush on her and let that cloud his judgment. Jackie apologized and promised he would not be hurt then ran to stop the alarm. Mark lay there, feeling like a complete fool, and he did not relish the moment when Helga would find him incapacitated in this way.

Meanwhile, Allison had broken into three of the file cabinets in Helga's office and was working on her fourth. Jackie ran straight to

Jack Franklin's office and busted open his one large file cabinet and dumped all the files into her bag.

As she was leaving, she saw the curious list on the corkboard and took that too. They were both back in the Porsche and racing down Wabash Avenue when she got her first text. It read: "I know it was you. Come back and discuss this mess immediately."

Of course Jackie ignored it. They believed they must have gotten out in the nick of time. They were barely a mile from the offices.

When the second text came fifteen minutes later, it read: "You and Allison have gotten yourselves into quite a jam. Return immediately or face dire consequences."

Jackie threw the phone out the window and floored the Porsche.

Back to the dock, Jackie left the keys in the ignition with the car running when they jumped on the boat. Hopefully the car would be stolen, and the tracker would take Helga on a wild-goose chase. As they moved away from the harbor, Jackie saw her beloved Porsche going in the opposite direction.

CHAPTER 68

Adrenaline was running high for the three, and Matt threw up a few quakes he should not have as he left the dock. He cruised as fast as possible down the river and entered the bay. Feeling a little more at ease, he entered the shipping lane and pushed the boat as fast as she could go. They would not feel safe until they were out safely in the middle of the Atlantic Ocean.

Hours later, exhausted mentally and physically, they decided to head up the Rappahannock River and drop anchor in a cove. Hungry, they cooked hotdogs and added chips before opening the first file.

The first file was mostly expense stuff, including the lease for the boat they were currently sitting on. Matt pointed to the GPS tracker portion of the lease and said, "I got that."

A few minutes later, he held the tracker in his hand to show the women then tossed it overboard.

"We won't be able to stay here long if the agency has already requested the tracking information."

They nodded and continued to go through files. Jackie opened her bag for the director's files. Here she found files with women's names on them.

She opened the first file on the pile which had *terminated* stamped on the front. There was a summary sheet:

> Franklin Project test subject name—Kelsey Angel Gutierrez
>
> Hospital—Harbor Hospital Center Born June 19, 1990, with addiction to crack cocaine

Payment agreement established July 7, 1990—
$300 monthly; $5,000 per incident

Payment name—Jesse Gutierrez

Subject address—29017 Cherry Hill Road,
Baltimore, MD

Number assigned—100

Date active—July 7, 1990

Date terminated—September 14, 2003

Payment agreement terminated December 31, 2003

Final payment $20,000

Jackie handed the page to Allison and read the next. It was a chart with entries handwritten chronologically.

June 23, 1990—contacted mother in Harbor Hospital Center parking lot and presented program.

July 7, 1990—mother accepted terms of agreement.

First payment issued. September 8, 2000

Location—home invasion

Level—1 Result—none noted

March 30, 2001

Level—1 Result—mild response

August 12, 2001

Level—2 Result—mild response

January 2, 2002

Level—3 Result—intermediate response

April 1, 2002

Level—4 Result—shock response

December 7, 2002

Level—4 Result—shock response

May 10, 2003

Level—5 Result—devastation response

August 11, 2003

Level—5 Result—devastation response

September 14, 2003

Level—5 Result—death by suicide

Jackie handed this second page to Allison, knowing in her gut that she, too, had a number. She looked at Allison. It had not yet dawned on her. She went on to page three.

Each of the dates listed on the front sheet were again listed with added details.

9/8/00—two assets, home invasion, pistols used.

Test subject removed from under bed and thrown on sofa next to other occupants. Fear noted. Guardian reported nightmares.

Payment issue date 9/9/00

10/12/00 guardian reported complete recovery.

3/30/01—two assets, for a street snatch.

Test subject grabbed and pulled behind a house. Her clothes stripped. Money taken. Subject screamed and urinated. Guardian reported to police as instructed. Subject traumatized.

Payment issue date 3/31/01

6/16/01 guardian reported full recovery.

8/12/01—one asset to be tempted into vehicle with candy.

Test subject taken to nearby woods. Subject screamed and was beaten then allowed to escape. Guardian not required to report to police. Guardian reported mild depression.

Payment issued 8/13/01

12/12/01 guardian reported full recovery.

1/2/02—two assets, abduction just off school bus/mild sexual assault.

Test subject taken to an abandoned house and forced to perform oral sex on asset one. Then allowed to escape. Guardian reported to police as instructed. Guardian reported subject is in shock.

Payment issued 1/3/02

3/1/02—Guardian reported progress but hesitation to leave home.

4/1/02—Guardian reported subject improved and recovered.

4/1/02—one asset, street snatch/rape.

Test subject taken behind an abandoned home and raped at knife point then released. Multiple lacerations inflicted. Guardian had discretion on police report. They declined. Guardian reported subject was in shock. Required stitches.

4/2/02—Payment issued.

8/09/02—Guardian reported inability to rebound.

11/1/02—Guardian reported recovery.

12/7/02—two assets, pipe assault.

Test subject attacked on street. Beaten with a pole. Kicked. Guardian had discretion on police report. They declined. Guardian reported subject in comatose state, unwilling to talk.

12/8/02—Payment issued.

2/1/03—Guardian reported subject wounds recovered. Mentally struggling.

5/1/03—Guardian reported subject may never be able to fully recover.

5/10/03—one asset, bedroom invasion scheduled for 3:00 a.m. Test subject woke to asset standing over her. She screamed. Mouth was taped. Hands and feet tied. Guardian entered room, and asset escaped back out through the window. Guardian reported subject traumatized.

5/11/03—Payment issued.

6/1/03—Guardian requested exit from program. It was denied as not part of agreement.

7/15/03—Guardian reported subject is angry and confrontational. Goal one achieved.

8/11/03—one asset, kidnap, and rape.

Test subject was abducted from her bedroom and held in an abandoned row home where she was repeatedly raped until allowed to escape a day later. Guardian reported extreme duress.

8/1/03—Payment issued.

8/20/03—Guardian reported subject admitted to hospital on suicide watch.

9/13/03—Guardian reported subject was released.

9/14/03—Guardian reported subject was found
in bathtub with wrists slit. Subject bled out.

9/16/03—Final payment issued. Subject terminated.

Tears were streaming down Jackie's face as she handed the
sheet over to Allison. Allison began to cry as she read the first entry.
Never had they imagined the horror they had both been through was
orchestrated by the agency they now worked for.

Allison finished the details sheet as Matt walked in.

"What?" he asked.

They handed him the file they had just finished reading.

"It is called The Franklin Project," said Jackie.

They then shuffled through the bag, searching for their own
files. Once located, they each read their own life stories as orchestrated by Jack Franklin.

Jackie was test subject 139, and her parents were paid about
$300,000 over the years. Allison said she was number 147 and worth
$190,000 to her foster father.

They further compared their files and were struck by the sim-
ilarity of attacks. They both had been pulled into an alley and their
clothes stolen as their first attack. At different intervals, they each
had been raped multiple times. And to their further astonishment,
their most resent street "test," the attempted robbery in Baltimore,
had also been orchestrated by the Franklin Project.

Suddenly, Jackie let out an anguished sob, stunned by all she
had seen in her file. She ran out on deck and vomited over the side,
sobbing uncontrollably.

Allison ran, also sobbing, and pulled her into a hug.

Matt broke the silence with "What the fuck is this?"

Both women looked down at Matt, their sobbing subsiding.

He asked, "Is this what happened to you two?"

Unable to speak yet, they nodded in assent.

"Jesus! How is this possible?" he said.

Suddenly understanding the depth of this sick project, Matt
became terrified.

In a higher-pitched voice, he said, "We need to get out on the ocean now. I'm pulling anchor, and we are going."

The women again nodded. Both were numb with the revelations their files had provided. They were also grateful that Matt had decided to help them.

CHAPTER 69

Matt navigated the Sea Beast down the remainder of the Chesapeake Bay and out into the open waters of the Atlantic Ocean. He took them a few miles offshore and away from the likelihood of being located. Thankfully the sea was calm this evening.

Matt let the boat idle and returned to Jackie and Allison. Their tears were now dry as they finished the count of "test subjects" Franklin had in his pool of candidates—fifty-four. Fifty-four young girls subjected to inhuman violence. It was the same number that was represented on the list Jackie had grabbed at the last minute from the corkboard in the director's office. They determined it was a cheat sheet of sorts, a list of all the women and where they were in the process.

Jackie and Allison did note that there were six who were still being terrorized. And worse, there were forty-two with the red T. They realized T meant "terminated or dead."

Anger then rage took over and was displayed all over Allison's and Jackie's faces.

Allison said to Matt, "Did you know our parents and guardians were paid to look the other way and allow these attacks? Our drug-addicted guardians cared more about their next fix than the welfare of their own children. In my case, the guardian and attacker were one and the same."

"Disgusting," Matt acknowledged.

He was feeling an enormous amount of empathy for the women. There was no way he could envision the hell they had lived through. He would do whatever he could to help reveal this project and protect the lives of others caught up in this nightmare.

There were other details being discovered in the files. Recruiters were used to go out and entice the test subjects to accept positions with the agency by placing signs where they would find them. They would be paid extra to befriend and advise the recruit to accept the position too.

But everything was so cryptic. The recruiters were not identified anywhere in the files that they could find. How did Franklin know who to give credit to for any of the indoctrinations?

They all took a break from the file reading and started talking about actions they needed to take. Matt had no hesitation in agreeing to help them plan the unraveling of the Franklin Project.

"We need a preplan before the plan to expose them," said Jackie. "We want to give Franklin a taste of the torture and terror we had to endure. Then we will turn the files over to the authorities and let them decide the fate of Helga and everyone else involved."

Matt did not like the sound of this, but he nodded all the same. It was their revenge to be had, not his. He would do more than sit back and let it happen; he planned to assist as needed. But he knew he was ill-equipped both mentally and physically to be of much use. He was not a trained assassin as they were.

CHAPTER 70

Their preplan was to abduct Franklin and bring him on the boat, so Jackie and Allison knew they must get Matt comfortable with the idea of witnessing torture. He was definitely not comfortable, but Matt heard out their plan and agreed.

These two women had killed before, and although he had doubts that they would harm him, he did not want to risk that either. They were too blinded by revenge right now. And besides, this Franklin dude really had it coming to him.

Matt had only read one file, but it was enough to make him sick to his stomach. And to know there were fifty-two additional victims? He shuddered. This man was a bona fide demon.

The women got to work devising a plan for the abduction of Jack Franklin, thoroughly researching any details they could find online. They knew there was no room for error.

They discovered that Franklin lived alone in his Finksburg, Maryland, home off Route 91. There was a write-up on the man behind the wildly successful Henderson Agency, and the pictures of his house on Turnbull Drive were detailed enough to take away some of the mystery of the interior.

Franklin portrayed a vain, pompous type of man in the article. They were quite sure he would think nobody would dare enter his home, much less abduct him. That would be his downfall. But first, they needed a distraction. Perhaps a ruse of extortion...

Having worked out the details of docking the boat on the Middle River, getting a rental car delivered there, and the subsequent abduction and return to the boat, the trio headed back toward the Chesapeake. They would once again need to refuel and stock up on food and supplies.

Heading north on the bay, they found a small marina in Hampton, Virginia that took care of both. They continued their journey toward the Chesapeake Bay Bridge and, hours later, entered the mouth of the Middle River. Matt pulled smoothly up to the dock and tied off the boat.

The women took the rental car and headed to Finksburg to case the director's home. They parked toward the end of Lawndale Road and jogged together through the neighborhood. Stopping to rest under the shade of a tree and drinking some water, they eyed up the mini mansion where the monster resided. They now felt ready.

CHAPTER 71

Helga and Jack met early that next morning after the break-in to do damage control. They had cameras in the interior of their offices, so they knew exactly who broke in and exactly what was taken. They were only in a mild panic, not sure yet of the women's intent.

They had six assets on alert and ready to deploy at a moment's notice. Helga had contacted the marina where the boat was rented and requested the GPS location but were informed the GPS failed somewhere on the Rappahannock River. She had dispatched two boats to search the Rappahannock without result.

The Sea Beast was nowhere to be found. They were now certain that Allison was the leak and that she had convinced Jackie to see things her way. They believed they also knew that it was to Carter Grayson that Allison had given those stolen details to. The elimination of the ten ex-employees did indeed handle the leak issue, as Helga hoped, when it revealed the letter writer.

The women had not yet reported them to the police, or they would not be sitting here talking. They concluded that it must be money as the phone buzzed.

"Sir, you have a call from Shelly Carson on line one."

Helga and Jack looked at each other knowingly.

"Yes, this is Jack Franklin," he said when he picked up the phone.

"This is Shelly Carson or Allison Kincaid, whichever your perverted mind wishes to call me. You know we raided your office and took some very sensitive information. If you want us to give it back, it is going to cost you. We will need enough money to leave the country and live on for the rest of our lives. Ten million dollars is our price along with five different passports each.

"We want the passports to be from the UK and the US. Will that be a problem? Or do you prefer to have a problem in another way?"

Helga's eyebrows shot up, and Jack whistled.

"That is a hefty price. Are you sure you girls want to go down this route? How do we know you will hold up your end of this deal?"

"We aren't the deceptive ones in this scenario. You are," replied Shelly.

"Can we have time to talk and get back to you?" requested Franklin.

Shelly laughed longer than she meant but answered, "No. You need to find it in your heart to agree right now."

Franklin exhaled a heavy sigh and said, "Okay, we will meet your demand. How and where do you want it delivered? But I warn you, if you double-cross us, you will end up as your friend Carter Grayson did."

Carter Grayson? thought Allison.

"Who is Carter Grayson?" she asked.

Helga and Jack looked at each other quizzically but responded, "So now you're innocent? We know you had been passing him information about the Franklin Project as well as assignments. Why do you think we polygraphed you?"

And now the pieces of the puzzle were sliding into place for Allison and Jackie. Helga and Jack thought that Allison was giving details of the Franklin Project to someone named Carter Grayson. That would be why they put a hit out on her.

Franklin was acting as though forfeiting a big win.

"We will call you back tomorrow afternoon with the details of the account to wire the money to and where to drop the passports. Then we will advise you of the files' location for retrieval once we verify the money is in place and the passports are in our possession," said Allison and hung up the phone.

"Okay, the ruse is in place," she said, and the other two smiled.

Franklin would be focused on that and not on an abduction in the middle of the night. So now they would wait until 1:00 a.m. to dock for phase two of their plan.

CHAPTER 72

Before they would continue their plan, they needed to know who Carter Grayson was and if he was still alive. They googled his name, and the news stories popped up about the home invasion and robbery that took his life. Grayson had also been a previous employee of Henderson and Associates before his retirement years ago.

Now they knew why. Grayson must have known about the Franklin Project and was trying to stop it. There must be another leak in the company, they surmised. But who? That was a question for later. Now it was time to get Franklin.

*****

The night was black, the pitch-black kind when there is no moon. It was a perfect cover as Jackie slowly drove the car without her lights to the end of Turnbull Street and parked. Allison made sure she had a round in the chamber of her firearm and headed toward the basement window of Jack Franklin's home.

They had already determined it to be the best point of entry on their run the day before. The window was small and made minimal noise as they busted it out. They both barely had enough room to squeeze through. No wonder it did not have an alarm sound.

They quietly crept up the steps to the first floor, where a small alarm went off as soon as they opened the door. Jackie quickly recognized and silenced the alarm. It was identical to the ones she used to use back at her old place.

They stood in absolute stillness for fifteen minutes to ensure the alarm did not arouse a sleeping Franklin. There was not a peep to be heard. Jackie stealthily began her ascent to the upper floor, taking notice of the open bedroom doors except for the one at the far end of the hall, the apparent master bedroom.

As a precaution, Allison checked every bedroom and verified their vacancy. Together, they burst through the master bedroom door to a sleeping and now startled, awake Franklin. He sat up in shock and stared at the two women standing before him, guns drawn and aimed at separate parts of his body.

This is not good, he thought.

He had not planned for this. He thought he knew their price. He conceded in his head he had slightly miscalculated their greed.

So $10 million would not be enough, he thought as he swung his legs to the floor.

He should have negotiated better.

"Good morning," Franklin said, sounding cheerful.

The women did not react. Instead, they instructed him to kneel on the floor with his hands on his head. He started to protest, but Jackie hit him with the stun gun.

"Thank you for complying without any difficulty," said Jackie sarcastically.

She secured his hands behind his back and put a gag in his mouth. Then they stood him back up.

They checked his pajamas for any type of concealed weapon and found none.

He truly did not anticipate this night could happen, she thought.

They walked him down and asked for his car keys. He nodded toward a hall table where both his wallet and keys lay in a shallow bowl.

Allison grabbed them both. They put Franklin in the back of his Lincoln Navigator and tied his hands to a bolt in the floor and then hog-tied his feet to his hands. He grunted in discomfort, and Allison laughed and said, "Enjoy," and she shut the hatch.

Jackie took off at a run to the rental car as Allison pulled out of the garage and closed the door with the automatic control from the sun visor. In and out and nobody noticed. Just as they had planned. The houses were just too far apart in this development for anyone to hear the noise of a break-in.

The cars followed each other back to the boat. It was 3:30 a.m. by then, and there was no activity at the dock as they opened the vehicle's hatch, untied his feet, and made Franklin walk to his fate aboard the Sea Beast.

Matt sprang to life with the first step upon the boat's deck. He turned on the motor then untied the boat and pushed off, adrenaline coursing violently through his veins.

The women put Franklin below at the table. They tied his feet around a steel post so he could not escape. Matt cruised the Sea Beast down the Patapsco River toward the Chesapeake Bay.

It would take time to reach the Atlantic Ocean again, so the women took turns napping. Only they knew it was to be a long couple of days ahead. Matt did not want to think about what was about to happen.

CHAPTER 73

The sunrise was magnificent. Matt was taking a break in Norfolk and gassing up again while he had the opportunity. He had no idea how long they would be on the water this time.

He stretched his arms and called Jackie over to show her how to steer the boat so he could take breaks.

"Once we are on the ocean, just keep us going east for about three miles. See the compass?"

"I got it," replied Jackie.

Matt jumped on the dock to fill up the fuel tank. Jackie had taken as much of a nap as she could. Allison still slept. Franklin was awkwardly slouched over and was snoring on the table.

Get your sleep now, Jackie thought.

Having finished with the fuel, Matt steered the Sea Beast back out into the bay then turned the helm over to Jackie to continue. Jackie took the wheel and Matt's advice.

"Keep her between the red and green markers and you'll be in the channel. It will take you under another bridge, and then we will be out in the ocean. And look out for the crab pots. That would bring this journey to an abrupt stop should you wrap the propeller up in one. The weather has nothing threatening on the radar and nothing forecasted for today, so we will be fine. But please wake me if you need to. Don't take chances if you are unsure of anything," said Matt.

Jackie assured him that she would not and that she could handle the boat. Matt dropped into sleep immediately. A few hours later, Allison woke and saw Jackie guiding the boat along.

"Nice," she said. "Didn't know you could captain."

"I can't really. Just keeping her steady while Matt gets sleep. We should be far enough out very soon."

Allison retreated to make some coffee and bagels and brought both up to Jackie.

"Franklin is still snoring. The man must be insane. Who sleeps so much when they've been kidnapped and don't know where they are going?"

Jackie agreed.

Matt added, "He will have one hell of a crook in his neck too."

"Good morning, captain," chimed in Allison. "Just made coffee. Want some? Bagel?"

"Both would be great. Thanks. How was the adventure?" he turned toward Jackie and asked.

"Smooth sailing," she replied.

Matt checked the GPS and said, "We are almost four miles offshore. We should stop here." He took the wheel from Jackie, put it in neutral, and turned off the engine. "Now what?" he said.

CHAPTER 74

Jackie walked down the steps to where Franklin was sleeping and hit him hard with her gun on the side of his head. He let out a groan and sprang to a seated position. Blood appeared through the small gash and began its trek down the side of Franklin's face.

She removed the gag.

"What was that, Jack? I couldn't understand you."

He started to talk but then closed his mouth.

Jackie could see his mind racing as he took in what was unfolding before him. He was a trapped animal, yet there was a cockiness about the look on his face.

Somehow he thinks he is still in control, Jackie thought and let a laugh escape her lips.

Allison asked if he knew where he was, and he replied sarcastically, "On a boat."

"Correct," she said. Allison reached under the table and untied his legs. "Why don't you come out on the deck and get a little sun with us?"

Franklin moved awkwardly with stiff legs toward the steps and walked out onto the deck.

"Sit there," Jackie said and motioned to a chair sitting in the middle of the stern side of the boat.

Franklin took in his surroundings, and alarm finally registered on his face. This was beginning to go the way Jackie had envisioned.

"Not another boat in sight, right, Jack?" she said, knowing that Jack had fully underestimated his predicament, and now they had his full attention.

Allison asked, "Can you swim, Franklin? It's going to come in handy if you can."

To their delight, he looked terrified at the idea of being thrown overboard.

"How about if your hands are tied?"

Franklin began to offer all kinds of money and reasons to not do this as Allison and Jackie grabbed opposite sides of his chair and lifted him up and over the side of the boat.

Jack screamed as he hit the water, pleading, "Please don't kill me this way. I've never personally killed anyone in the program."

The women looked at each other and replied, "We will have a conversation and make a decision on that. Hold tight."

Franklin struggled to keep afloat. He flailed and went down and popped back up several times over the course of about fifteen minutes. Matt kept an eye on him and signaled with his hand that it was time to come get him.

The women returned with a boat hook and said, "We talked it over. You are correct. We won't kill you this way," and they pulled a choking, grateful man out of the water.

He pulled himself up over the side and fell onto the deck.

"Allow us to help you up," said Allison as she dug a grappling hook into Franklin's buttocks and pulled up.

He howled with pain.

"Oh my. I'm so sorry," she said. "Don't worry, salt water heals everything."

Jackie appeared with boiling hot salt water and said, "Let me sear that wound for you," and poured it over the cut from the hook.

Franklin sat whimpering, and Jackie put a towel around his shoulders.

"There, there, Jack. You will heal. We will check in with your guardian and see how you are progressing," she said. "Captain," squawked Jackie, "how is the test subject progressing?"

Matt responded, "He appears to be adjusting well to his situation."

"Excellent," replied Jackie. "On to level two."

CHAPTER 75

Franklin looked up with horror in his eyes. It was evident that he finally understood it was revenge that they were after, not money.

"We have only just started," Allison whispered in Jack's ear. "This one will be for Carter Grayson. You should know, I have never met the man. You have caused everything that is about to happen."

Franklin looked doubtfully at Allison.

"It's true. Had you been smart enough to realize that I was not the leak you were trying to find, you would not be here. We would have been none the wiser of your evil plan."

Franklin began with apologies at his mistake. He offered them their freedom, free of prosecution if they released him without further harm. He promised he would not report them to the police. But even as he spewed the words, they both knew the declaration was not genuine.

Allison approached Franklin with scissors.

"Stand up," she commanded, and Franklin rose.

She cut off his pajama pants, and he began to tremble as the pieces pooled around his feet.

Jackie grabbed his penis and yanked as hard as she could. Jack fell forward and curled into a ball, whining.

He sounds like a sad coyote, she thought.

They again ordered him to stand up and cut his pajama shirt off and let it lie where it fell.

Allison cracked the pipe wrench against Jack's ribs, causing an audible break. Again, the coyote howled but in shorter gasps this time. She continued to crack his body with the pipe down his left arm and left leg, preserving the other side of his body for Jackie.

Once Allison was done, she handed the pipe wrench to Jackie. Jackie decided she wanted their torture of Jack to drag on a little longer and opted instead to kick his other side. She laid the pipe wrench down next to his head for him to see as she finished the torment with a kick to his ass.

Together, they dragged him back into the chair and tied him in place.

CHAPTER 76

Franklin had passed out. They left him with hopes that his skin would burn in the sun.

Later, as the sun set, Jackie lifted an icy pitcher of salt water over his head and dumped it. He shuddered into consciousness. His skin was reddened but not quite yet burned as they had hoped.

"What do you think, guardian?" Jackie asked Matt.

"Completely recovered," he responded.

"Excellent," said Jackie. "On to level three."

Allison stepped up with broomstick in her hand. Franklin's face went white. He could figure out what was coming next, which caused him to pass out again. They decided to let him sleep for the night and resume in the morning. They were not yet ready for him to be completely broken.

At the front of the boat, they relaxed in chairs and replenished their bodies with food and drink. It was evident that Matt was barely holding on, clearly agitated at what he had just witnessed. He sat in another seat and exhaled loudly.

Jackie began, "We're sorry, Matt, to have dragged you into this. We didn't know at the start this would be where we were headed. We are so incredibly grateful for your help. It looks ugly now, but there is an end to this, and when we get there, you will not be implicated in anything. This man deserves what we are dishing out and more. We hope you can continue to help us through to the end."

Matt stared at the two and nodded. Jackie and Allison knew he understood; he had read the files of what Franklin had done to them and others. He needed to be stopped, and the torture was excessive, but they wanted to retaliate for a lifetime of needless attacks. They would continue until they felt closer to vindication, believing Matt would be okay in the end.

CHAPTER 77

The dawn was muted, but the sun burst through by noon. The women were initially disappointed that Franklin would not get excessively burned this day with all the clouds, but they would continue their plan.

Up on the back deck sat a now fully awake Jack, who croaked a few words of apology as they approached.

"I'm so sorry," he said. "I only wanted to develop the best assassins under disguise the world has ever seen. Women with incredible inner strength and trained abilities to work without being suspected."

As though Jack never uttered a word, Allison untied the prisoner and said, "On your knees, subject."

Franklin refused.

"I really, really hate repeating myself," she replied.

Still he did not budge.

Jackie unsheathed her knife and dragged it down his belly, stopping just short of his penis.

"Your choice," she said.

Franklin started to cry as he slowly knelt on the deck.

"Spread your legs wider," demanded Allison, adding to the humiliation they were doling out.

Franklin vomited.

Allison had no mercy and rammed the stick into his rectum.

"Ever wonder what it feels like to be raped? Well, now you are finding out."

She continued until her rage waned and then passed the stick off to Jackie, who continued until Franklin could only whimper.

They left him lying on the deck with the stench of his shit and vomit, cuffing his hand to a rail. They retreated to the other side of the boat for the rest of the day. Darkness was settling in, and they hoped his mental suffering was as great as the physical suffering they were inflicting.

But of course, they were not yet done. Tomorrow, they would continue. Though they were coming awfully close to their own limits with his torture. They decided on going inside for the night.

CHAPTER 78

They passed beers all around, not in celebration but more as an exhausted end-of-day ritual. Their moods were very somber with a feeling of emptiness.

They all needed a break from the brutality and took their time finishing the beer in silence. They closed the door to keep the smell out as best as possible and ate sandwiches.

Jackie knew this was still a lot for Matt and asked how he was doing.

He replied, "A little nauseated to be honest. Not so good. I am not used to this level of violence, but I do understand the need to exact your revenge. I am quite sure I would react the same way if I were in your shoes. I will be okay."

Jackie took his hand and pulled him into a hug and apologized and thanked him again.

The torture was a lot for Jackie, too, but she kept the facade of being hard for Allison's sake. She knew Allison needed to exact every little piece of revenge she possibly could. She knew she needed Allison's bravado to help her feel vindicated as well.

The two had a weird sense of balance in this. Allison with the guts to do what Jackie really wanted to do. Jackie pulled along to do those things by Allison's side.

CHAPTER 79

They were operating on little sleep now, but Allison felt like it was time to continue, so they returned to the deck and hosed it down. The vomit had dried up into a hard substance, and there was the excrement from the last round with the broomstick that would need to be washed off the deck.

Matt picked up the broomstick and threw it overboard. He could not stomach to see it any longer. Allison trained the hose on Franklin's face to wake him.

"Rise and shine, buttercup. No, wait. You need a new name. Let's see. Your new name will be Eustace Peckersucker. Mr. Peckersucker, please return to your chair."

She unlocked the cuffs so he could comply. Franklin was terribly bruised and weak but managed to drag himself up into the chair.

"Guardian, how is your subject this fair morning?" she asked.

"Right as rain and good to go. Completely healed," replied Matt.

Franklin groaned.

"Excellent. On to level four we go."

Jackie tossed a knife to Allison and then unsheathed hers. Franklin screamed before he was even touched, which prompted a laugh from the women. They dragged the knives over his skin as he howled in pain.

Undeterred, they continued until they had carved fifty-four sets of initials into his skin, saving theirs for last. They carved those deeply into his face. Blood ran in every direction on the deck, and Matt kept the hose handy to keep it from running below deck.

"Oh dear," said Allison. "I think we may need more salt water to help heal his wounds."

And with that, Jackie wrapped a rope around his legs and tied it tightly. They tied the other end to the side rail and once again flipped the chair up over the side of the boat and watched Franklin's bloody body dip into the ocean.

They heaved him back up and said, "Do you think the sharks might like this blood?" and dropped him back in, dunking and pulling him out a half dozen more times and adding remarks to encourage his fear.

Only because they were tired did they pull him out for the final time. Surprisingly, Jack glared at his torturers in a silent threat. Then he lay on the deck, and the three took a break for a few hours.

CHAPTER 80

Sounding the boat's air horn next to a sleeping Franklin's ear, Jackie shouted, "Guardian, how is the subject healing?"

"I believe he's suicidal. I think he should withdraw from the program."

"That was not an option presented in our contract. Will the subject completely heal?" Jackie asked again.

"Then yes, the subject will and now is completely healed," replied Matt.

"Fabulous. We have reached level five."

Jackie turned back to Franklin. "Time to sit in the chair again, big boy," she said.

Franklin heaved himself up and fell backward, adding an additional gash to the back of his head. It bled profusely.

He tried again and made it to the chair by his third attempt. Jackie tied his feet to the chair and untied his hands. She held out a cup of water to him.

"Would you like a drink?"

He nodded and reached for the cup.

Jackie pulled it away out of his reach.

"This is mine," she said and drank it down.

Franklin was severely dehydrated and trembling and could barely talk. He was badly sunburned at this point, and his eyes were beginning to swell shut. Surely his head had to be pounding. His whole body was hurt badly from the beatings and assault.

Jackie open handedly smacked him across the face to bring his focus back. They could not have him passing out again and missing the finale. Franklin opened what he could of his swollen eyes but seemed to pass out again.

Jackie broke smelling salts open and waved them under his nose. He became alert, and Allison added another slap for good measure then picked up the pipe wrench.

"You know, this can end one of two ways, right?" Jackie said as she set a knife on his lap. "By your hand, which would be the easy way. Or by the pipe wrench hand, the hard way. Your choice."

Allison smacked his kneecap with the pipe wrench for emphasis.

"I will never kill myself. I am not weak," he replied.

"That's the answer I hoped for," said Allison as she swung the pipe onto his shoulder.

He whimpered in the way of the coyote again, and his body convulsed. Jackie waited for the convulsion to end.

After he returned to consciousness, she then took the knife and stretched his penis out and, in one quick motion, castrated the demon. She returned the knife to his lap and thanked him for the loan of it.

She waved his bloody penis closely in front of his face then threw it overboard.

"It was useless anyway," she said.

Anger taking over, Franklin took the knife in his hand and slashed weakly at Jackie. "You will not get away with this."

Franklin had lost quite a bit of blood, and the women were surprised he could still talk.

"Sure, we will. The files will be turned over to the proper authorities, and your disappearance will be attributed to escaping the fallout. It will be assumed you are on the lam."

Franklin considered what to him seemed her slurring words and felt hopelessness wash over him. He wanted to rest his eyes but was scared to close them.

Matt lit a cigar and handed it to Allison. She approached Franklin and put it between his lip to smoke. He choked some. More because of how dry his mouth was than because of the actual smoke. She extinguished the cigar on his neck. He barely made a sound, clearly beyond feeling.

Franklin looked up at the women, then he looked at the knife lying on his lap, and without further thought, he raised the knife and slit his own throat just before he most probably would have passed out again.

The three exchanged looks with one another, unsure of how they felt now that the revenge was complete. They stood there in the quiet as they had done the first night this had begun and took the scene in.

Franklin appeared as a fraction of the big man they had known. Jackie advanced and untied his legs. The three quickly picked up his body and threw it overboard.

Deciding to put an unequivocal end to the events of the past few days, they continued to clean up the evidence and bleached down the deck, each showering with the hose and soap before throwing their clothes overboard too. When done, they had effectively erased Jack Franklin from the face of the earth.

The women sat out on the deck and cried. They cried in relief. They cried for loss. They allowed their grief to completely pour out.

Jackie and Allison cried such a long time that they realized that Matt looked worried. Had they had lost their sanity? The whole ordeal was incredibly horrific. No one would ever be the same.

Matt pushed the Sea Beast to her limit on their return to the Chesapeake Bay and soon passed under the first bridge of the Bay Bridge Tunnel. Just after the bridge, he pulled to the left and docked at Little Creek Marina where he paid for a slip to stay the night.

They all retreated inside and locked down the boat so no unwanted guests could enter. Matt cracked open beers for everyone and asked how they were doing. They shrugged, both still raw from the revenge they had just exacted.

It felt so right while it was going on, but once the adrenaline had dried up, they were spent. Matt suggested they all get some sleep after the beer, and they would continue in the morning with the rest of the plan.

The women slept closely against each other, and a restless Matt kept vigil as though the demon could rise from hell. He turned off their alarm clock so that they would sleep in. They needed the rest and the peacefulness it offered.

CHAPTER 81

"Dammit, Jack, this is no time to ignore me," said Helga loudly.

They were supposed to meet again for the money wire transfer information this afternoon, but he was not in his office and not answering his phone.

She worried he would hang her out to dry and not pay. She checked the company account for the third time this morning. Nothing appeared to be missing. The balance was still at healthy $476,000,000 she expected.

She remained stoic outwardly but was anxious inside. She sent out the texts to deploy assets as she usually did. She had Emily and Oscar take the bags and envelopes to assets in the Baltimore hotel. She went on about her day as though nothing was different.

Helga was not prepared for the hell that was about to break loose in just a few days' time. Absolute control had always been her guiding principle, and she could not fathom a lack of control over Jackie and Allison. She conceded that they may have some control temporarily, but that would change.

As soon as it was determined where the girls would escape to, she would designate the assignment to one of the newer assets who came onboard to the covert side to perform the elimination. Those new assets were the ones eager to please. They would not let Helga down.

Helga dialed Jack's phone again. He still would not answer. She threw her phone across the room in frustration.

The following morning, Helga began to wonder if something else had been going on. It was highly out of character for Jack to be nonresponsive for more than a day. She drove by his home and knocked on the door. Again, no answer.

She dialed his number from the porch to hear if the phone rang inside, but it did not. Helga did not know what conclusion to make. She was too fearful of alerting the authorities, as the deal to secure the Franklin Project files was not yet completed. She reluctantly decided to wait.

By the third day, Helga could no longer conceal her anxiety. Mark asked if there was something going on that he could help her with, but Helga just walked toward her office in a confused daze without a word.

Mark was also puzzled as to the disappearance, but in his gut, he knew Jackie had something to do with this. The office turned into a buzzing, crazed feeling after the break-in the other day. He phoned the admiral to update him on the current state of affairs at Henderson and Associates.

CHAPTER 82

After a long night's rest, the three began the final part of their plan. They would have breakfast before they called the number listed for the nearby NCIS location in Norfolk, Virginia. They requested to meet with a senior investigator, as they had devastating evidence they needed to turn over.

NCIS agreed to send over an investigative officer to speak with them. Giving them their location at the marina and boat slip number, they hung up and waited. What seemed like hours but was only forty-five minutes later, an investigator, Lieutenant Harry, arrived and called out to them as they lounged on the deck, drinking coffee.

They invited him aboard and down below to sit at the table and read the files they had selected along with the tally sheet from Franklin's corkboard. As the investigator read about the Franklin Project, his concern grew large. He first read the file of the original victim and her subsequent suicide.

Troubled, he opened the next file to read the details of Caron Tucker's childhood, and his mouth dropped open. Harry was completely stunned such a project could exist. He completed his reading with the details of her current life as Jackie Ford.

The investigator started gathering up the remaining files. Already he had reached his limit with reading the details of this real-life violence. He excused himself to get his wits collected, then returned, and asked, "How did you come by these files?"

They explained their break-in at the agency but, of course, omitted the part where they abducted and killed Franklin. Harry wanted to be sure he understood the situation.

"So you realized something was not right when an order came for Jackie to kill Allison," he said, pointing to each woman as if to clarify their identification.

"Yes," they replied. "Every assignment we ever undertook is in our files. If you check Jackie's file, you will see the order to kill. Allison was her last assignment."

Lieutenant Harry opened Allison's file. He picked up the fake death picture of Allison and asked, "So this, I'm guessing, is not real?"

"It is not" said Allison.

Harry was reeling as the enormity of the information in his hands became evident.

"I must admit to you that this is above my pay grade. We need to call my supervisor and include him in on this and determine how we should proceed."

Harry folded the files and placed them in a pile then dialed his commander.

"Sir, you need to see this immediately," he said.

CHAPTER 83

Commander Rosen ordered Lieutenant Harry to return to the office with the files and the three people he had met. They agreed, knowing they would eventually have to face scrutiny.

They were escorted to a conference room and heard the door lock click into place. Suddenly scared, they sat and waited for whatever was to come next. What happens if the Navy would want to do a cover-up and they were expendable?

Their nerves were now completely shot. A couple of hours later, the commander called them into his office, and they were invited to sit at a round table there.

*****

Rosen was a man with a precise demeanor. Everything about his person was in perfect order—pressed and creased uniform, shined shoes, gray hair perfectly trimmed, and no facial hair. He appeared to be about sixty but in perfect shape.

Rosen sat down at the table and shuffled then straightened the files in his hands. He could hardly look at the women, but when he did, there was deep apathy in his eyes. Rosen cleared his throat and began.

"So you two are Caron Tucker and Shelly Carson?"

He pulled their files and placed them on top of the pile he had just quickly read through.

"Yes, we are," they replied.

"On behalf of the US Navy, let me be the first to apologize for the atrocities you were forced into. Henderson and Associates is known in the upper ranks of the US Navy as a well-run covert intelligence operation with the security agency as its front. I can assure you that the Franklin Project was not sanctioned. It appears that Jack Franklin was rogue in this program."

"That was exactly what we thought," said Shelly, visibly relaxing, as they were unsure how deep in the government the program ran.

Rosen continued, "I have alerted Quantico of this situation, and they have already dispatched an investigative team to the Baltimore offices of Henderson. The program has been suspended, and all assets have been recalled."

Matt smiled and nodded. The women squeezed the hands they were holding and once again, tears flowed.

Rosen continued, "On behalf of the US Navy, I would also like to thank all three of you for your heroism in obtaining these files safely and turning them over to us. It was the right thing to do. Not everyone would have done the right thing. If you should need anything, *anything*, do not hesitate to call me directly."

He laid out three cards in front of them.

"Now can you start from the beginning and tell me exactly how this came about?" he continued.

Not knowing where to begin, Shelly started with Caron's appearance in her hotel room in Tijuana.

Once the floodgates were opened, the information flowed, each ridding themselves of a poison inside, each releasing the anguish that all the knowledge of the Franklin Project had brought them.

CHAPTER 84

Later, when they returned to the boat, the three were able to finally celebrate their victory. The ordeal was completely over. They mindfully put their own brutality behind them and decided to just live going forward using their original identities.

Captain Matt had cruised out into the open bay waters once again and decided to try to catch some dinner. He was pleased as he managed to haul in a couple of fish. He was currently cooking them on the deck grill as they passed around a bottle of tequila.

The music blared loudly. Caron had taken care of that and, once again, chose Queens of the Stone Age. Shelly turned the music down after a few songs so she could speak.

"Jac...Caron, I want to toast you. You saved my life. I am so fortunate that in her sick mind, Helga thought it a clever idea to send you for my assassination."

Caron just hugged Shelly.

"We did say we would have each other's back way back in training, right?"

"Hear, hear," said Matt, raising the bottle to his lips then passing it around again.

Caron and Shelly cried once again, and the tears suddenly turned into laughter.

"Let us truly move on and be happy," Caron toasted back.

They finished the tequila and started in on the remaining beer as they slowly made their way north and then anchored in a cove near the Potomac River. Matt confessed he was too drunk to go on.

They fell asleep on the deck, not wanting their night to end. On their minds was a little unfinished business that the women had not shared with Matt. They agreed to discuss that list sometime after they returned to dock in Annapolis.

CHAPTER 85

Matt felt it before he heard it. Drops of rain hit his face as his prone, hungover body came to the realization it was raining.

No, it is storming, he thought with alarm and sat up quickly.

The boat was bouncing around, but the anchors held her firmly. He shook the women to get up and go beneath for protection from the lightning. They would have to wait the storm out.

Caron and Shelly lounged back on the cushions around the table as Matt started the coffee and switched on the television. The six o'clock news was just starting.

"Breaking news overnight in Northwest Baltimore. A security agency called Henderson and Associates was raided"—and they showed Helga being perp walked out in handcuffs—"Early details show the agency was operating as a drug front with Jack Franklin and Colleen Seamon in control. Ms. Seamon, as you can see, has been apprehended, but Mr. Franklin remains at large. If you have any information on his whereabouts, please call the Baltimore police department. He is considered armed and dangerous, the police say. Lin, back to you."

Forgetting their hangovers, the crew aboard the Sea Beast cheered loudly.

Then laughing, Caron said, "Helga was really Colleen Seamon?"

It did occur to Shelly that Helga could be a victim too. But they did not see a file on her from Franklin's office. Maybe she just chose a name to feel like she fit in. That might be a mystery never figured out.

"Wow. Drugs though. That is how they will play this then," said Matt as he handed coffee all around.

"What else could the Navy do? They would not want to embarrass themselves or risk the intelligence network being discovered. In Baltimore, a drugs story works well," said Shelly.

True enough, thought Matt.

CHAPTER 86

Matt dropped the women back at the Annapolis dock. The women were going to miss Matt. Caron and Shelly spoke quietly of the scars they had dealt Matt and hoped he would fully recover and be his old self.

Matt had also become their champion and friend, and they did not want to lose touch, so they exchanged their goodbyes and keep in touches before parting ways. Caron rented a car, and feeling safe now, Shelly wanted to visit James in Baltimore right away. She needed to see him and had Caron drive her there.

Shelly also wanted Caron to meet the man who took her in and hid her from Franklin and Father Tony, the man she loved most in the world. James was far more of a father than any of the foster homes she had been through.

Caron could see why Shelly loved James. It was apparent in his eyes that he loved her too. They embraced, and Shelly brought Caron inside to visit and meet the rest of the crew in the gym.

They stayed there for most of the day then headed to the hotel where Caron still had a room in Jackie's name. The two ordered a ridiculous amount of food and beer from room service and ate until they thought they would burst.

They wondered how high they could run up the hotel room tab before they were cut off. They never were. At last they fell into a solid, rejuvenating kind of sleep and did not wake until noon the next day.

After the fun of the previous night, the women decided to go for a run and work off some of the extra calories they had no business eating. They decided on Charles Street for their run and raced each other up about five miles before turning and racing straight back down the hill.

It was a run of freedom. Freedom they had never experienced before in their lives. Nothing would dictate their lives from this day forward. It was not so much voiced as it was felt.

They walked back up Pratt Street to cool down and entered the lobby of the hotel. For a moment there, Shelly thought she saw Father Tony and was ready to pounce. But she was wrong. How long would she look over her shoulder?

As they rode the elevator up, she decided she was glad it was not him. She and Caron had big plans for a few more people, including Father Tony. That revenge will come later on her terms.

CHAPTER 87

Not ready to part ways, the women remained in the hotel room for several days, enjoying their newfound freedom and talking about potential future plans. They considered opening a true protection agency but also offering training geared toward women protecting themselves. They were putting their ideas down on paper when the phone rang.

Caron answered, "Hello?"

The number was blocked, so she had no idea who it could be.

"This is Commander Rosen again. How are you ladies doing today? Is Shelly with you?"

"Yes, she is," replied Caron.

"Can you put me on speaker so I can talk to the both of you at the same time, please?"

Without a response, Caron hit speaker on her phone.

Shelly said, "Okay, we are on speaker. What can we help you with?"

"Well, since you put it that way," said Rosen, "you can help the United States government by accepting the appointment of directors of the Blocker Agency in Boston, Massachusetts."

The women did not respond.

"Hello? Did I lose you?"

"No, we are here. We are just surprised at the request. What exactly does this job entail?"

"Well," said Rosen, "first and foremost, integrity. We need to keep a covert intelligence operation in place for the east coast. There is already a network of assets waiting for reassignment after the Henderson debacle. Only there will not be any secondary programs involving women ever again. We need someone to take over and lead this segment of our government back into the light. It surely has seen some very dark days lately. Who better than the two bravest women I've ever met?"

Again, the women were speechless.

The commander continued, "Okay. Cat got your tongues?"

"No, sir. This was just very unexpected," said Caron.

She turned to Shelly and asked with her eyes.

"Can we think it over? Can you e-mail us the particulars?"

"Of course," said Rosen, and he took their information and said jubilantly, "Welcome aboard!"

"But we have not accepted yet," said Shelly.

But the commander had already hung up the phone.

The commander was feeling crumby about his role in this affair. He was genuinely taken by surprised when the program was revealed to him. When he took it up the chain of command, he was given instruction to not let this go anywhere further than his office.

He was not to share any details with anyone anywhere or at any time. He felt the gravity of the situation and agreed it would not serve the country well should the information become public knowledge.

They also needed to contain Shelly Carson and Caron Tucker in a way that would prevent them from exposing the information in the future. The admiral would formulate a plan and get back to the commander to help deliver it, which was what they did this morning.

They decided to relocate the Henderson Agency to Boston and rename it the Blocker Agency. They would have to put the women through training before they were to take command of this important agency, but the positions should be offered without delay.

So that was what the commander did, and now he was e-mailing the details of the job and the training required before they relocated. He genuinely hoped they would be okay.

Unlike Harry, Rosen had taken the time to read all the information the women had handed over. It was staggering, mind-blowing. How this went on undetected so long was beyond his belief.

Someone knew something but did not do a damn thing to stop the insanity. Rosen was smart enough to keep those thoughts to himself. In fact, he would keep all the details of the Franklin project to himself. He prayed that Franklin himself would never return.

CHAPTER 88

Caron and Shelly wanted to tie up some loose ends before they began training for their new assignment in Boston. The positions offered were surprising but exciting. They fully intended to run the business, as it should be run and rid of all traces of Helga and Franklin.

Their revenge plans were designed to be simple. Complex was something they both agreed to avoid given the long ordeal with ending Franklin's life. So, on one sweltering summer day, Caron and Shelly walked in the front door of Bill and Sonya Tucker's home.

It took a moment to register that this was their daughter standing before them. Sonya exuded happiness and greeted Caron with a hug.

"Where have you been all these years?" Sonya asked.

Bill seemed unable to speak. Half of his face looked droopy, and Caron recognized he had the signs of a stroke.

"Oh you know, Mom. I've been off killing the bad guys. I am quite good at it, being you helped me early on with my training. It was nice to see how much I was worth to you."

The color drained from her face, and Caron realized it did from her father's as well.

"I'm here to thank you," she continued and saw Sonya brighten, but it then turned to confusion.

Caron did not care; she had long ago lost love for her parents. Shelly restrained Sonya, and Caron leaned down to her mother, kissed her on the cheek, said goodbye, then slid the sharp blade of her knife over Sonya's throat.

Her father watched with an expression of horror on his face. It would not be necessary to restrain Bill. He was not able to get himself out of his chair. Caron walked over to her father and slapped him as hard as she could across his face.

"You should have protected me, not sold me," she spewed then slit his throat too.

The women tossed the house and took jewelry to complete the appearance of a home invasion gone wrong. Once completed, they strolled out the same way they came in as if nothing out of the ordinary had just occurred with Caron allowing the screen door to slam for the final time.

*****

Shelly had previously visited Tony right before she left for training with the Henderson and Associates Agency. But that visit was no longer satisfying enough, given the information that came to light about his part in her "training."

Tony had been paid hundreds of thousands of dollars—just like Caron's parents had been—to put Shelly in harm's way for years in an effort to toughen her up for the Franklin Project. Shelly knocked on the old familiar door and saw Tony peek out from behind a stained yellow curtain.

She was well aware he would never let her in, so she busted the small window on the door and reached through to open the lock and gain entry. Shelly brushed the glass from her jean jacket sleeve and entered the house with Caron on her heels.

Tony had retreated upstairs, scared, and was hiding behind a curtain in the shower. Shelly ripped the curtain open and ordered him out. Tony initially refused until Shelly produced her knife and again made the request.

She watched Tony carefully exit the shower and move toward the hallway, walking with an exaggerated limp as though decrepit.

"Downstairs!" Shelly ordered.

Tony slowly proceeded to the next floor down.

"Keep going," she again ordered.

Tony looked at her with pleading eyes and said, "Why are you doing this? Didn't you already have your revenge? Please don't put me in the basement."

Shelly laughed. "Perhaps there is something left over in the vault to provide comfort for you."

Shelly had frequently been locked in this vault as a young girl until she ran away as a teenager, sometimes with men or sometimes as an unreasonable punishment for a nonexistent transgression.

The women marched him into the vault and removed everything within that could be of comfort or help. This time, Caron held the monster while Shelly slowly slit his wrists to ensure he would bleed out. They closed the vault door and turned the cylinder so that Tony could hear the audible click of the lock, as Shelly once had in the past.

They proceeded back upstairs to stash heroin and OxyContin behind a picture on a shelf behind the worn-out sofa in the living room. Five thousand dollars was placed haphazardly in a drawer in the kitchen to help solidify the notion that Tony was a drug dealer.

They patched the front door with a piece of old cardboard, designed to look like it had been there for months. They swept up the glass from the smashed window to take with them. Just before they exited, knowing enough time had passed that Tony should be dead, Shelly headed to the basement and opened the vault door.

Tony was propped in a corner in a pool of his blood, eyes closed and skin flaccid. Satisfied, Shelly closed the door again but left it unlocked. The two women exited the house, carefully locking the door and pulling the cardboard piece in place over the window.

CHAPTER 89

Caron returned to the gym to see Reggie and Mike. It had been so long since she had seen their friendly faces that she rushed to Reggie and hugged him straightaway. Reggie was happy to see her and called out to Mike to come from the back.

"Look who the cat dragged in," said Reggie.

Mike beamed. "Well hello, stranger. How are you? How is the job going?"

They, too, embraced.

The three sat and chatted, and Caron caught them up on her job. Only she told them she was promoted to Boston and omitted everything about the Franklin Project. She felt grateful to these two men for helping her when she most needed them.

"I honestly don't believe I would be going to Boston if it hadn't been for you two with the excellent training. Hell, I may not have even taken the job had you, Mike, not given me that little push. I felt like I should give notice, not quit on the spot at the grocery store. So thank you both!" Caron said.

Reunion complete, Caron needed to do one more thing: break into her old apartment and get the stuff she stashed under the old floorboard in the kitchen. She waited until she knew the apartment was empty and went in.

The apartment made her feel nostalgic for a moment. She pulled a knife from her pocket and cut into the super glue to pry the board up. She reached in and got the contents and shoved them in her pocket before replacing the board. Quickly she exited.

Back on the street, she put her social security card and the money in her wallet. She looked at the knife and smiled, knowing she now carried a much more effective weapon but kept it all the same.

She opened the flyer that had started the process and read it once again, recalling the call she had made that first time to the Henderson Agency. At the bottom, she noticed the letters *MH* under the number.

Those letters had been important to report. Why? What did they mean?

CHAPTER 90

Caron met up with Shelly later that evening and told her she had completed everything with her old life and she was ready to enter training for the Blocker Agency. Shelly was looking forward to this and moving on with her life. They both desired to live fear-free and happy.

Caron showed Shelly the flyer over dinner at Sabatino's, a restaurant in the Little Italy section of Baltimore. They shared a huge pasta dinner and a bottle of red wine.

"Remember this?"

"Holy shit! You still have that flyer?" was Shelly's response.

"I had tucked it in the floorboard of my apartment with some other things. Who knew what it would come to mean?" said Caron.

"Well, it is worthless now," said Shelly.

"I am not so sure. Do you remember being asked what the letters under the number on the flyer were?" asked Caron.

"Yes. So?" she replied.

"What do you think it means?" asked Caron, hoping to put their heads together to figure out the mystery.

She pointed out the letters at the bottom of her flyer.

"Do you suppose it was a way to figure out who the recruiters were for each asset?" asked Shelly.

"Could be. Do you remember the letters from your flyer?"

"I don't," replied Shelly.

"In the notes we found from the Franklin Project, it said something about paying recruiters for their level of involvement with getting the asset to come on board at the agency. I am thinking this was the way they tracked that," said Caron.

And then the sudden realization knocked the breath out of her.

Could it be?

No. She would not give in to paranoia. No way. She did not want to believe what she was thinking, but it did make a little sense.

Caron looked up at Shelly and said, "MH is at the bottom of this flyer. It could be Mike Heller, my trainer. He was a Navy SEAL. Oh my God."

Caron paused to think, and Shelly took her hand in support.

"I think you are right. It does make sense, and he is Navy."

Caron began to cry with the deep hurt within her heart.

Mike meant the world to her. He had guided her through the toughest of times and prepared her physically to defend herself. All the while he was secretly preparing her to be a government-sanctioned assassin.

It was Mike who talked her into accepting the position so quickly. It was Mike who went over every scenario of how to better defend herself after each attack. It was Mike who shaped her into the killer she was now.

This hurt way more than what her parents had done. Mike had her complete trust and exploited it for his own gains. Caron was not done with her old life yet. She would have to take care of one more thing before reporting to training.

CHAPTER 91

Caron and Shelly both agreed that Mike Heller would be a hard target to kill. Their plan would have to be more creative and more careful than what they had done previously. Shelly urged Caron to reconsider, as a Navy SEAL's death would absolutely draw attention.

Caron would not let this go. She believed it only meant they needed to carefully construct a plan. They needed to figure out something foolproof that would not draw attention.

Shelly gave into Caron's need for revenge. She fully understood and decided to help in any way possible. They began with surveilling Mike to get an idea of his routine.

Mike had a rigid routine. Most days he would go to the gym and work out before it opened. Once Reggie arrived, they would open to the members. Afterward, he would pick up dinner somewhere before returning home.

Occasionally he would meet with a woman at a bar for drinks. They followed the couple back to what they believed to be the woman's home and waited. Two hours later, Mike emerged then headed back to his own home.

But on Thursday mornings, Mike deviated. He would go over to Martin State Airport instead of the gym and meet up with another man. The two would go through the motions of checking each other's gear that was lying on the ground in front of them. Parachutes, oxygen tanks, harnesses—all labeled with their names—would be checked thoroughly.

They would then take off in a small plane which disappeared into the sky. Later their parachutes would be visible as they floated to the ground. They seemed to be going up to a high altitude before jumping.

Caron researched on the Internet and figured out that they were indeed jumping from high altitudes, and that was why they had oxygen tanks. The process of checking was done to ensure all the equipment was ready for the jump, which included a full tank of oxygen.

A seed of a plan was emerging. What if instead of oxygen, the tank was filled with carbon dioxide? It would provide for an accidental death scenario. A scenario that should not draw too much attention.

Caron went to the airport and inquired about skydiving. She told the woman who greeted her she had heard that she could jump here and wanted to know about the process. The woman took Caron on a tour of the facility and showed her the process.

She noticed there was an area of open lockers with names written in black marker above the top shelf. She scanned the names until her eyes rested on Heller. It was here that he stored his gear for jumping out of plane.

Caron walked toward the gear and asked, "Would I have to have my own gear?"

"No," replied the woman. "That is gear that is used by regulars who come here to practice."

Caron really wanted to get a closer look at the oxygen tanks.

She took her phone out and asked, "Do you mind if I take a picture? This looks intense and cool all at the same time."

She took the picture before the woman could respond, but she finally said, "I'm not sure if that is allowed."

"Okay," said Caron, and she put her phone back in her pocket.

They finished the tour, and Caron said she had to consult her husband before signing up. She thanked the woman and left the facility.

Back with Shelly at the hotel, Caron showed her the pictures of how the oxygen was labeled and stored. They talked out the details of switching oxygen for carbon dioxide and settled on how they would execute their plan. First, they would need to buy an old oxygen tank.

They located a tank and purchased it empty from a scuba shop outside of Baltimore. Taking it back to their room, they began the process of making it look identical to the one in the picture. Satisfied, they next had to fill the fake tank with carbon dioxide.

Following instructions they found online, they purchased an air compressor to fill the oxygen tank. First, they put the tank into a cold bath to keep it cool and prevent it from exploding in their faces. It would also ensure there were no bubbles and thus, no leaks.

Then they headed down to the garage, thankful it had open air on each level. They started the car and put the air compressor next to the exhaust pipe to pull in the carbon dioxide. They had taped a piece of duct to the exhaust to funnel it directly to the tank and allow it to draw in the maximum amount possible. Next, they attached the yoke to the tank and allowed it to fill until the automatic mechanism shut it off.

The oxygen tank was now ready to be switched out with Heller's at the airport. They stowed the tank and the compressor in the trunk. The next part was going to be the most challenging portion of the plan.

Shelly walked into the airport and asked questions in the same manner that Caron had. This was designed to get the attention of the employee at the front desk focused solely on Shelly. Brochures were opened and jumps explained.

Meanwhile, Caron was carrying the oxygen tank around the side of the building to enter the door nearest the lockers. She had donned a ball cap and clothing to appear male, as she knew there were cameras alongside the building.

Once inside, she quickly swapped tanks then headed back the way she came. The cameras would see her carrying the same tank both ways and hopefully, if viewed, make her appear to be a lost customer. She loaded the tank in the trunk of her rental vehicle as Shelly exited with brochures in her hand.

The plan was set. Now they had to wait a day for Mike to show up and go skydiving. Caron and Shelly sat in the hotel bar and drank until it closed.

CHAPTER 92

As Caron and Shelly ate a room service breakfast, they watched the news. They were waiting to hear the report of the skydiving accident that took the life of Mike Heller, but nothing was reported. After the noon news also had no report of the accident, they began to doubt that their plan had been successful.

They decided to go for a run toward Patterson Park to help with the anxiety. They would loop the perimeter then head back to the hotel. The two felt in limbo; everything halted until they had confirmation that they succeeded in their plan to kill Mike Heller.

They picked over dinner and barely ate as they watched the evening news. Still there were no reports, and their anxiety level rose. What if he figured out his tank had been tinkered with? What if he knew it was a different tank?

The worry continued through the night, and the next morning, they could not eat until they went to the gym to see if Mike was still alive. Panic almost set in because Caron knew she would be on Mike's list of people. He would figure out that she knew of his role in the Franklin Project.

Mike was not in. They were not yet ready to breathe a sigh of relief because he could be biding his time somewhere until he figured out who swapped tanks. They trudged back to the hotel, unsure of what their next move should be.

They ordered a late breakfast and switched the TV on to wait for the noon news. They needed to consider what to do in the event Mike came looking for them. Where could they hide?

It became a moot point because the noon news opened with the story.

"Breaking news from Martin State Airport," began the anchor. "There has been an accidental death of a Navy SEAL doing continuing skydiving certification.

"Michael Heller was last seen as he jumped from his plane on Thursday morning with his partner who is also a Navy SEAL. The two routinely performed these exercises at the airport, but Heller did not land in the designated area as usual.

"Police scoured the area and located his body this morning about a mile west of where he should have landed. It is unclear what happened, but sources say his parachute was not deployed. More to follow as details emerge in this developing story."

Caron would have preferred an ending with Mike where he knew exactly what happened. She wanted him to know that she won in the end. She would not have that luxury because she could not afford the consequences that would have come with it.

Caron began to cry, and Shelly said, "Thank God."

Now it is done, thought Caron. *It is really done. No more unfinished business.*

"I think it is time to call Rosen and start training" was all Caron could say.

Shelly looked sadly at her friend. They had both been through so much trauma that they needed this fresh start, and the training would give their minds something to concentrate on.

They could now move on.

CHAPTER 93

Six months later, Shelly said good morning brightly to the security guard at the front door as she scanned in her credentials to access the secure building on the outskirts of Boston.

"Good morning, Director Carson," replied Mark.

Mark had been reassigned to the Boston field office by the admiral. To his utter amazement, he had managed to come out of the Baltimore office unscathed. No one suspected he had anything to do with the Franklin Project, nor did anyone know of his dealings with Carter Grayson.

Carter, he read in the paper, had been the victim of a break-in, robbery, and murder. Mark thought he might know the real reason for Carter's murder but knew to speak up was to reveal his double life, so he kept silent and feigned ignorance whenever possible.

He feigned ignorance about everything when he showed up to guard the Boston office too. Here, he would continue to surveil and report to the admiral, but otherwise the program would be sanctioned and legitimate.

Mark already had the offices bugged well before the new directors had arrived. He was further directed to gain their trust by any means possible.

"It will be very important in the coming months. Perhaps years," explained the admiral.

A few minutes later, Caron scanned her badge through security and said, "Good morning, Mark."

"It is indeed," replied Mark and winked at Caron.

She threw him a stern look before smiling and continuing to her office.

Caron and Mark had an ongoing flirt thing since he was stationed in Baltimore, and Caron decided to go a step further and ask him out. Their chemistry was instantaneous. They had been together three weeks now and barely stayed out of bed.

My life has decidedly taken a turn for the better, she thought.

She passed her own office and went to Shelly's, where she deposited a cup of coffee on her desk. Today, it was her turn to pick up the coffee from the Dunkin' on the corner.

"Good morning, Director," she said.

And Shelly smiled broadly and replied, "Good morning, Director."

ABOUT THE AUTHOR

Debrah Dennis was born and raised in Baltimore City. She faced challenges in her life, which she used as inspiration to write this, her first novel. She currently resides in Westminster, Maryland, though her heart remains in Baltimore.

CPSIA information can be obtained
at www.ICGtesting.com
Printed in the USA
BVHW080626110921
616280BV00001B/37